A WREATH FOR THE BRIDE

A WREATH FOR THE BRIDE

by

MARIA LANG

translated by

JOAN TATE

HENRY REGNERY COMPANY · *Chicago*

Published in Sweden 1960 under the title
Kung liljekonvalje av dungen copyright © 1960 by Maria Lang

English translation copyright © 1966 by Hodder and Stoughton

First published in the United States 1968 by
Henry Regnery Company
Library of Congress Catalog Card No. 68-31461
Manufactured in the United States of America

Main Characters

ANNELI HAMMAR	the heroine
GRETEL STROM	the mother
EDWARD STROM	the stepfather
JOAKIM CRUSE	the fiancé
DINA RICHARDSON	the friend
SEBASTIAN PETREN	the employer
LEONARD LARSSON	the admirer
MATTHEW NORRGARD	the stranger
FANNY FALKMAN	the florist
LEO BERGGREN	Police Superintendent
ANDREW LOWE	Police Inspector
CHRISTER WICK	Chief Inspector

Chapter One

THE month was June. The day was Friday, and the time, according to Dina Richardson's admittedly somewhat unreliable statement, was ten minutes to three when she was halted at the corner of Priest Street and River Street by someone calling her name. She turned round and screwed up her eyes against the sun in surprise.

'Why, Anneli, it's you. Darling, I was just thinking about you. Where have you sprung from? How are you? Are you nervous?'

If the inhabitants of Skoga had not had twenty-five years in which to become used to this attractive constellation, then they would have had good reason to slow down and take a closer look at these two friends. Since childhood they had been opposites. While Dina was and always had been lively, talkative and full of *joie de vivre* and mischief, Anneli was quiet, self-absorbed and a dreamer. Accordingly, Dina had providently been equipped with brown curls, at present extremely short, a cheeky nose and laughing slanting eyes, while Anneli was slim and fragile, a classic beauty of romantic pallor, her very fair hair caught in a graceful chignon at the back of her head. To all appearances, however, they got on very well indeed with each other.

Anneli sighed briefly and said with a slight grimace: 'I've been to the hairdresser's. Mother thought it'd be better if I had it washed today because . . . because then the head-dress would be easier to fix on. And of course I'm nervous. Heavens above, what on earth am I letting myself in for? Summer wedding in Skoga church – it sounds lovely – do you remember how we used to dream about it when we were at school? You were always going to marry a lieutenant, and I was going to have a big, safe man who was at least six feet tall . . .'

She stopped with a treacherous catch in her voice, and Dina, who had always been afraid of sentiment, pointed out somewhat dryly: 'And now you've nabbed the richest bachelor in the whole district. And all the girls are green with envy, and all the mums are furious, and tomorrow the whole town will be in church or crowding round outside to criticize you, so no stumbling or stuttering or blushing, but just look happy and thrilled and in love, for this is the WEDDING OF THE YEAR in this hole, and everyone already knows you're going to wear a genuine lace veil that's two hundred years old which once belonged to Joakim's mother, and that there'll be champagne for eighty people and you're spending your honeymoon . . .'

'For heaven's sake, stop! I've already told you, I *am* nervous. The funny thing is that it's Daddy and I whose knees are wobbling most. Both Mother and Joakim seem to be enjoying the spectacle in some unnatural way.'

She thrust her arm under Dina's and they walked on down River Street. Anneli's white cotton dress stood out brightly against her friend's red one, one girl carrying a white bag in her hand and the other a red umbrella.

'I'm just going to Falkman's to look at my bouquet. Joakim's orders. He says I've got to "approve" it.'

'What on earth has he thought up, then?'

'Oh, roses, I suppose.'

Anneli sounded indifferent and absent, but a moment later she was waving her hand and smiling happily at someone behind a window.

'It's Len. No, there. In the barber's. He must be sprucing himself up for tomorrow too.'

They swung round the corner into Little Street, past the expensive new tobacconist's and stopped at a shop window stuffed with carnations and green cucumbers.

Dina screwed up her impertinent nose.

'The way she does her window. No, I'm not coming in with you. I'm allergic to Fanny Falkman. I can't stand her untidy hair or her endless talk. I'll wait out here, but try to get her to understand that you're in a *hurry*.'

And with that Dina nodded carelessly to her best friend and watched the white frock disappear into the florist's shop.

A cloud covered the sun. It was thick and greyish black,

8

and she congratulated herself on her foresight in bringing an umbrella.

At that moment she caught sight of Livia and Olivia Petren purposefully making straight for her. She hurriedly deliberated whether Fanny Falkman's more businesslike chatter were not preferable to that of the Petren sisters, but she had not managed to make up her mind before they were there.

No one looking at them would believe that these two sixty-five-year-old ladies belonged to one of the best families in Skoga. Olivia, plump and bulging, was wearing a tight-fitting flowered artificial silk dress, its shiny surface billowing and surging at her every movement. Livia, thin and dry, had found in one of her wardrobes a lilac-coloured hat which had probably been created round about the time of Dina's birth, and from under its brim her eyes peered, as inquisitive and shrewd as a squirrel's. As usual, both of them talked at once.

'Well, well, good morning, good morning, dear Dina. How are your mother and father?'

'Are they still in Italy? Well, that *is* a pity, now, isn't it . . .'

'Just now, with the wedding and everything. Yes, we've had an invitation. Dear little Anneli has worked for so long in our office, so I suppose she thought . . .'

'Olivia means that she was employed in *our brother's* office. We have nothing at all to do with Sebastian's office or his affairs. No, that we cannot say, even if he did once take it over from dearest Papa – but naturally it was kind of the Stroms and Anneli to remember us on their big day . . .'

'I think it's going to rain,' said Dina hopefully. 'Perhaps I'd . . .'

'Oh dear. Yes, you'd better mind that hat, Livia. But let's move off the steps and stand in the entrance for a while. It'll probably only be a shower. There was one like this yesterday, such a heavy one it knocked all our lupins flat, but it didn't last for more than five or six minutes . . .'

Dina put up her smart umbrella and smiled politely, but she stayed on the pavement in full view of the entrance of the florist's shop, and as the rain pattered on the red silk and her

9

feet got wetter and wetter, she glanced impatiently and expectantly at the shop door. Wasn't Anneli ever coming? And wasn't there any way of stopping these two old girls talking?

'Oh my goodness, what a lovely bride she'll be. Mrs Persson is making the wedding dress, and I can tell you, it's going to be wonderful, but of course there are eighteen yards of material in the skirt . . .'

'But it's a shame old Doctor Hammar didn't live to see this day.' Livia shook the lilac-coloured hat sadly. 'But one must admit she couldn't have had a nicer stepfather, and she needed one too, for that poor muddled Gretel Hammar could never have looked after either herself or the girl. And won't they look handsome walking up the aisle . . .'

'Oh, yes.' Olivia rapturously clapped her stubby hands together. 'You can easily see that his mother was of the English nobility . . .'

'I was talking about Edward Strom,' said Livia sternly. 'As the father of the bride, he'll be the one to lead her to the altar.'

'But there he'll be relieved by the bridegroom, won't he?' Olivia tittered, as if she had suggested something improper. 'You know, when he picks up that monocle of his and fixes it in his eye, it makes me shiver, for then he looks like . . . he really looks like . . . can you guess, Dina?'

She leaned forward confidentially and whispered her question with flushed cheeks. And Dina, who in common with the three thousand other inhabitants of Skoga was well aware of Olivia Petren's secret passion, at once decided to be a little friendly and accommodating.

'It couldn't be . . . ?' she whispered back. 'It couldn't possibly be . . . *Lord Peter Wimsey*?'

Olivia clucked blissfully, and she became even more enraptured when the object of her admiration appeared on the corner by the tobacconist's. He seemed to be in a hurry, but all the same he stepped politely up to greet the little group in the entrance.

Dina Richardson looked at him thoughtfully and noted again as she had so often done during the last six months that she did not know what she really thought about Joakim Cruse.

He was not bad-looking. Perhaps he was a shade too thin. His hair had an unmistakable red tinge; in addition it was cut in that idiotic way which had once been modern and relatively suited to young boys, but which was hardly appropriate to a man of thirty-five. But his light grey summer suit was faultlessly cut, as was his pale blue striped waistcoat (Joakim always wore a waistcoat, whatever the weather or the temperature), and even without his monocle he gave an impression of self-assurance and elegance.

Sometimes he's silly, thought Dina, as he is now, standing in the rain kissing those two old dears' hands, and sometimes I wonder if he's all there, and yet ... and *yet* ...

'Yes,' she said aloud in reply to Joakim's appeal. 'Yes, she's in Falkman's. I think she'd be pleased if you went in to fetch her. She must have got stuck in there.'

He bowed three times, once for each of them, walked the short stretch to the florist's steps and opened the door. They heard the doorbell tinkle as he was swallowed up in the dim foliage of the shop.

Suddenly it stopped raining as swiftly as it had begun. Livia said goodbye abruptly and hurtled on towards the market. Olivia, who would have very much liked to remain and discuss the interesting Mr Cruse, followed her reluctantly. Dina Richardson put down her umbrella and decided to tell Anneli that she was not going to wait any longer.

It was cool and dark in the shop, and there was a smell of earth, vegetables, carnations and roses. Fanny Falkman, large and black-haired, was standing behind the counter at the far end of the shop. In front of the counter stood Joakim, and when he saw Dina, he turned towards her and uttered three short words, which in their simplicity were quite unbelievable.

'She isn't here.'

Dina stared stupidly and repeated his words.

'Isn't ... isn't she here?'

Almost impatiently, he shrugged his shoulders.

'Mrs Falkman says she hasn't even been in here.'

Dina was seized by a peculiar sense of unreality. Her eyes darkened.

'But . . . but that's impossible,' she mumbled. 'I saw her vanish through the door. And I've been waiting outside all the time . . .'

It was almost frighteningly quiet. The three people in the shop seemed to be holding their breath.

Then Dina made a helpless gesture, and although she did not understand why Anneli should want to play such a game of hide and seek, she made a tentative suggestion.

'She must . . . she must have gone out another way. Is there . . . is there a back door?'

Her heart sank as she looked at the florist, whose eyes were serious and implacable, holding no promise of such an easy solution to the problem.

'To get to the back door,' Fanny Falkman said slowly, 'you have to walk straight through the store-room. And I've been in there for the last sixty minutes.'

Chapter Two

FROM that astounding moment the mystery was a fact. The mystery which was to perplex and agitate Skoga more than anything else in its hundreds of years of history, the mystery which was to end with two funerals instead of a wedding and which was to give the town's most famous son, Chief Inspector Christer Wick, his first grey hair.

However, he was as yet still quite unaware of all this. He had felt tired and listless during the drive from Stockholm, and he had wondered whether it was worth sacrificing two days of his holiday for a wedding, when he did not know either party very well, but then Anneli was his own mother's goddaughter, and if there were one woman for whom he had a permanent weakness, then it was his mother. So his disinclination vanished as soon as he had, with considerable difficulty, swung his black Mercedes through the narrow gateway of the Wick home and contentedly noted that all was as usual; the lawn, which needed cutting, the long low house with its peculiar brown colour and white balconies, the almost finished jetty down by the lake and first and foremost the dignified owner of the whole. He almost lifted her off the ground as he hugged her.

'You get younger and younger,' he said happily. 'How old are you, exactly?'

'I've got my pension this year, you know. I have lots of money every month. It's very nice.'

They smiled at each other, and although his eyes were bright blue and hers as brown as chestnuts, and although she did not even come up to his shoulder, the likeness between mother and son was striking. They had the same smooth black hair, the same high forehead and also the same friendly ironic twist of the lips and the same clever, slightly penetrating look in their eyes.

With his arm round her, Christer walked round the house.

'You obviously don't use your money to pay a man in the garden, then? You need one here.'

'I've got a man,' said Helena Wick.

'But,' she added thoughtfully, 'I'm not sure he'd be any good at cutting grass. And it doesn't matter anyhow, for I like it as it is.'

Christer looked curiously at the gable window on the ground floor of the house. Behind it was a flat — two rooms and a miniature kitchen — which Mrs Wick usually rented to a lone educated woman.

'Yes, of course, you wrote and told me that you had a bachelor for a change. The bridegroom of tomorrow, isn't it? Joakim Cruse . . .'

Later that evening, after Christer had eaten a meal of home-made brawn, pickled herrings and steak and onions and had drunk three cups of his mother's speciality — black coffee — he filled his pipe, and leaned back in his favourite chair.

'A bit of gossip, please now, Mama,' he said. 'What's he like, this man Anneli's going to marry? Is he good enough for the child of your heart?'

Helena sighed.

'I wish I could answer that. He's of a very good family, Scottish aristocracy on his mother's side — and that perhaps explains a good deal — and he's said to be immensely wealthy. He came to the town in November after buying the coat factory . . .'

'So he's that rich, is he? That's quite a firm. But he's relatively young, isn't he?'

'He's thirty-five. If one follows the old rule that says the husband ought to be ten years older than the wife, then the auspices are singularly favourable . . .'

'You're prevaricating. Why? Come on, out with it, Mama. We've never had any secrets between us, have we?'

Mrs Wick had let her sewing drop into her lap. She screwed up her dark eyebrows as if she were puzzling over some unsolved riddle. Then she suddenly laughed at her own broodings.

'The worst of it is that there aren't any secrets. There's

14

absolutely nothing but a vague and general impression that he is . . . what can I say . . . *unusual* in some way. Different from the others. You never really get near him . . . I even wonder if Anneli has . . .'

'Hasn't she confided in you? Is she in love with him?'

'I presume she is. Why otherwise would a modern girl rush off and get married? . . . Yes, I see what you're thinking. But not Anneli. She's quite indifferent to money.'

Christer Wick searched his memory and picked out a few momentary images from past holidays in his home town.

Anneli at seven or eight years of age with long socks and blonde corkscrew curls, delightedly jumping round her father, the kindly, good-natured Doctor Hammar. Anneli as a worshipping teenager with huge blue eyes and exalted ideas about God, the Universe and Love. Anneli two summers ago, a grown woman already, with a transparent, exquisitely beautiful face and a gentle, slightly otherworldly disposition. And she was always together with Councillor Richardson's retroussé-nosed daughter . . .

He had just reached this point in his thoughts when the stairs up to the first floor creaked and Dina herself stuck her dark page-boy head between the curtains.

'Hullo, Aunt Helena. Welcome home, Christer.'

As he unfolded his long legs out of the armchair and achieved a greeting, he sensed the surprise in himself. Had she always been that pretty? Had she undergone a metamorphosis, or was it just he who had never noticed her before. Appreciatively, he registered one detail after another: the strange slanting brown eyes, the piquant oval face, the perfect figure under the scarlet cotton dress, the well-shaped legs and ankles. But it was doubtful, however, that she was fully aware of this appreciation. For once Dina Richardson was thoroughly put out.

'It's crazy,' she exclaimed emphatically. 'The whole story is mad. It's nine o'clock and no one has seen a sign of her, and it's not at *all* like Anneli, and what can one . . .'

'Sit down,' said Helena Wick, 'and calm yourself. And do start from the beginning. What has happened?'

Dina did not sit down. She leaned against a walnut

chiffonier and said: 'Anneli has gone up in smoke. *She pranced into Falkman's the florist's at about three o'clock and disappeared.* Open Sesame. Like a rabbit in a hat.'

Mrs Wick threw a swift searching look at the girl, saw how pale she was under the sunburn and reached out for the coffee percolator.

'Strong coffee is good for budding hysteria. I've brandy in the sideboard in the dining-room. Bring it, Christer.'

Dina smiled weakly and sat down on the sofa.

'You'd be hysterical too, Aunt Helena, if you'd had such an afternoon. I, who was going to have my hair done and get some beauty sleep. Poof!'

She took a few sips of both the coffee and the brandy which Christer had put down in front of her. After that she did not even seem to be aware of his presence. She brushed her hand over her untidy curls and straightened her dress at the knees.

'I just couldn't stay at Lake House. Aunt Gretel keeps nagging and buzzing and worrying, and that unbearable Joakim seems to want to blame *me* for everything. As if I could be responsible for his fiancée leaving him in the lurch on the day before the wedding.'

'Is that what she's done then, do you think?'

Christer's eyes met hers and held them. She flushed slightly.

'That's the only explanation,' she said. 'Not that I can see how it happened or why she should want to . . .'

Christer re-lit his pipe and repeated his mother's question: 'What happened exactly?'

Dina had explained what had happened several times during the afternoon. To Anneli's mother, to Anneli's father, to Anneli's fiancé and then again to the mother, father and fiancé. She was to repeat it several more times to various representatives of the local police and the State police. The man listening to her at the moment was no less than the head of the Stockholm Crime Squad. But afterwards Dina thought that he had been the easiest to tell, the one who listened most calmly, the one to extract the most details out of her. And yet none of them had any idea that this informal interrogation was the introduction to an extraordinarily involved and trying investigation into a murder. It was simply Christer

16

Wick's nature to be thorough about a case, whether it turned out to be small or large, a bagatelle or of considerable significance.

'I met Anneli in town,' Dina began, pulling out a packet of cigarettes. 'She said she'd just been to the hairdresser and was going to Falkman's to look at her bouquet.'

Christer leaned forward with a match. She's got a lovely skin, too, he noticed.

'What time?' was what he said aloud. 'And where did you meet?'

'Outside Mattson's shop.'

'At the corner of River Street and Priest Street, then?'

'Yes, and I should think it was about ten to three.'

'You'd think. What makes you think that?'

'Well, I'd been shopping in Eckman's. That took at least half an hour, because I tried on a girdle and then we talked of this and that . . .'

'Are you certain what time you arrived at Eckman's, then?'

'Well, no, not exactly *certain*, but . . .'

'In other words, you might just as well have met Anneli at half past two as just after three.'

She peered at him through the cigarette smoke.

'You're horrible. I didn't know I was going to be third degreed.'

'Third degree is much worse. This isn't even first degree. It's a kind of preparation for children and inconsequential ladies.'

Innumerable small creases appeared on her nose when she laughed.

'I went with her,' she continued. 'We walked down River Street and went round the corner by the tobacconist's.'

'Did you meet anyone?'

'No–o.' She hesitated and suddenly remembered something. 'But we saw Leonard – Len Larsson, you know – he's our best friend, and is going to be best man tomorrow. He was sitting in the barber's and Anneli waved at him.'

'No one else? Was the street quite empty?'

'No, of course it wasn't. But we didn't see anyone else we

17

knew . . . Well, then we stopped outside Falkman's window . . .'

'The shop's just opposite the wine shop, isn't it? And quite a bit on from the corner to River Street?'

'Yes, the whole of the tobacconist's is in between. Anneli went in and I waited outside . . .'

'Why? Didn't you want to see the bridal bouquet?'

'Not to the extent of enduring Fanny Falkman. She talks you to a standstill. And I can't understand why she can't brush her hair occasionally.'

Christer turned to his mother, who had watched his little display of the technique of interrogation with amusement.

'Old Man Falkman's dead now, isn't he?'

'Fanny's been a widow for three years. But she's looking after the business on her own, and very well too. Though I agree with Dina. She's very vulgar and difficult.'

He nodded to Dina to continue.

'Well, I waited quite a while.'

'How long?'

'Quarter of an hour or so. There was a heavy shower. And then the Misses Petren appeared.'

Helena Wick noticed her sigh and smiled.

'Then you did fall out of the frying pan into the fire!' she said.

And Christer added maliciously: 'Presumably you were chatting away so eagerly that you didn't notice Anneli leaving the shop.'

'Certainly not,' replied Dina indignantly. 'The Petrens just nattered on, but I was only listening with half an ear, and I was looking out for Anneli all the time so that she could come to my rescue.'

'Where were you standing?'

'At first we were standing just by the steps into Falkman's, and then we moved into the entrance, about four or five yards further on, and I was never actually *inside* the entrance . . .'

'It's one of those wide covered entrances of wood which lead into the yard inside, isn't it?' asked Christer.

Mrs Wick confirmed this.

18

'One of the oldest in Skoga. The yard was part of an inn in the sixteenth century.'

Dina's voice was very serious as she went on.

'I had my face turned towards the florist's all the time. And if there is anything certain in this uncertain world, then it is that no one could have gone into or come out of that shop without my seeing them.'

'And the entrance behind you? Could anyone have gone through that?'

'Impossible. We were standing there blocking the way.'

'Were there many people in Little Street?'

'There was quite a regular stream in and out of the wine shop, and a number of other people, of course. Then Joakim came.'

'From which direction?'

'Round the corner by the tobacconist's. He spoke to us and then went on in to Falkman's to fetch Anneli.'

'How did he know that she was there?'

'He'd told her to go and inspect that blessed bouquet. He asked me whether I'd seen her, and I said yes, she was in Falkman's. And so he went in, and then it stopped raining and then I got tired of waiting and went after him to tell them so.'

There was a second or two's pause, and her eyes reflected the disbelief and confusion she had experienced at the time.

Christer sucked at his pipe.

'And Anneli wasn't there?'

'No one was there except Joakim and Fanny Falkman.' Now the words poured out of her at such a rate that Christer had no time to put questions. 'Fanny protested that she hadn't seen a sign of Anneli and when I implied that there must be a back door, she said that you'd have to go right through the store-room to get there and *she had been in the store-room for the whole of the last hour.* Joakim was annoyed and superior and silly and said I'd been having hallucinations and had imagined that Anneli had gone into the shop. And then he stuck that monocle of his into his eye and went off into the store-room to admire the bouquet. It was a giant spray of lilies-of-the-valley, and they were marvellous,

19

but I wasn't in the mood to admire them and instead quite definitely annoyed old hag Falkman by searching her shop and store and W.C. as well as her private flat. On top of that, I rushed through the town like a madman and frightened Anneli's parents out of their wits. Joakim appeared after a while, and I was so horrible that I was pleased when she hadn't appeared either for dinner or for evening coffee. Him and his hallucinations.'

'It's all very strange,' said Mrs Wick slowly. 'Anneli goes in through the door of a florist's, she doesn't come out through this door again, but a quarter of an hour later she has vanished without even setting foot in the room which leads to the yard entrance. One is almost tempted to turn to the occult for an explanation.'

'Oh, well,' drawled Christer, 'one doesn't have to be a spiritualist to guess that Fanny Falkman is lying.'

'No,' said Dina hesitantly. 'But *why* on earth should she do that? After all, it's a little difficult to believe in the white slave traffic on Little Street in Skoga.'

He gave a light shrug of his shoulders.

' Perhaps she promised Anneli to say nothing. She might possibly have simply been paid to do so. You yourself thought that Anneli had simply decided to run away from her bridegroom.'

But in the illogical way of women, Dina had already abandoned that theory.

'Never. She'd never wish to bring such misery to her mother and father. Nor to Joakim either for that matter . . .'

'I'd got the impression that Joakim . . .'

Christer's ironic tone of voice was replaced by Dina's impatient one.

'Now you're being stupid. All I said was that *I* thought him unbearable. I shouldn't want to spend a honeymoon with him for all the tea in China, but Anneli and I have always had different tastes, and there's no doubt *she* wanted him.'

She stubbed out her half-smoked cigarette and added a trifle acidly: 'Anyhow, she's much too conventional to cause such a scandal quite voluntarily.'

And Helena Wick, who was optimistic by nature, said

calmly: 'Perhaps she felt a need to be alone for a few hours in the afternoon in the middle of the fuss. If she isn't back yet, she'll probably turn up before the wedding.'

This friendly assurance caused Dina Richardson further anxiety.

'Good heavens,' she cried. 'It's past ten and I haven't done a thing. I'd better be off.'

Christer rose with a smile.

'Are we so uninteresting?'

She looked at his tall figure searchingly.

'I wouldn't put it that way.'

He did not offer to see her home. The Richardsons' house was next door and he thought it would seem much too solicitous.

But Chief Inspector Wick's dreams that night were not about Anneli Hammar and her mysterious visit to the florist's but about a dark woman who had Chinese slant eyes and a hundred wrinkles on her nose when she laughed.

Chapter Three

HELENA WICK let up the blind in her son's room and put the tray of morning coffee down.

'Mmmm,' said Christer sleepily. 'It's obviously gorgeous weather for weddings.'

Mrs Wick sat down on the edge of the bed and waited until he had taken the first gulps of the steaming coffee.

'Yes,' she then said slowly. 'But the question is whether there will be a wedding.'

He was suddenly wide awake.

'Anneli? Hasn't she . . . ?'

'No. They haven't heard a thing from her. Christer, you've got to do something about this. Things aren't right.'

She was deeply troubled, and he did not point out that the person or persons who should 'do something about it' were the local police and not him. Instead he was out of bed and ready shaved before the coffee had had time to cool. He drank it and ate a couple of sandwiches, tying his tie at the same time.

'I'll go over to Lake House,' he announced.

Helena nodded in approval.

'Poor Gretel will need all the consolation and help she can get. She sounded quite distracted when I spoke to her on the phone. And no wonder. Anneli is her only child, and it's only natural she should be worried stiff. It's not much fun imagining the mighty scandal that's brewing either. It's exhausting just to think about all the gossip it's going to cause in town.'

Christer had got no further than the gateway when he realized the truth in that statement. Four housewives were either on their way to or from the market on this lovely Saturday morning, but they were not in such a hurry that they had not time to stop for a few minutes, put their heads together and pronounce excited comments.

'Yes, it's quite true. They say that she had a terrible quarrel with that fancy fiancé . . . and then she was off . . .'

'Yes, indeed, we know what men like that are. He's a foreigner too, they say, a count or a baron or something like that, and he has his dinner regular at the hotel, and our Anna, she says she's never served such a queer cove . . .'

'Monocle and all . . .'

'But it serves Gretel Strom right, stuck-up and affected like she is. I've often almost *wished* . . .'

Christer Wick walked the short distance past Mr Richardson's lilac hedge and had almost reached Anneli's home when he heard a 'psst!' behind the fence on the other side of the road. His height allowed him to look over the yellow fence and there he saw a red-faced elderly man with quite a considerable paunch peering at him through a pair of gold-rimmed spectacles. The man padded up to the fence and whispered cautiously: 'Have they . . . have they found her yet?'

Christer bowed.

'How are you, sir. It's a long time . . .'

He saw that Sebastian Petren had become more prosperous every year. To judge from his figure it was obviously a good thing to be a successful businessman, a wealthy bachelor and a bigwig in the town. The high colour in his face bore witness to dangerous tendencies to stress and high blood pressure.

Sebastian did not wait for a reply to his question.

'How are things . . . will there be a wedding?'

And immediately after that he added: 'Incomprehensible! Such a nice pleasant girl. I'll miss her in the office. Has she run away?'

'She's said to have gone into a florist's . . .' began Christer.

But Sebastian Petren interrupted him with surprising swiftness.

'Wagging tongues. I thought you police didn't listen to that sort of thing.'

The telephone bell suddenly rang from within the ugly but expensive house. He excused himself with a certain relief and hurried across the lawn. Christer Wick stayed for a moment, but when Petren did not reappear, he went on to the real object of his walk.

Lake House was the last of the fine old private houses down

23

by Lake Skoga; farther on were only fields, the summer colony and market-gardens. The house was one of the sights of the town; a long one-storey building of stone faced with white plaster, which had been built by a rich landowner called Hammar at the end of the eighteenth century, and which both externally and internally had some of the famed classic simplicity of the country houses of the district. There was not a single planted tree on the whole site. Ancient giant maples and chestnuts gave plenty of shade and almost completely hid the view over the water.

When Anneli's father had been alive, Lake House had been 'the doctor's house', beloved by all the inhabitants of the town; his widow had stayed on there after she had married Edward Strom, a confident and humorous businessman in the timber trade, a few years younger than his wife. Although he did not come from the district and had moved into the town as recently as 1945, he had been accepted surprisingly willingly as one of the townspeople and at this time had even been elected on to the town council. Christer knew him and appreciated him as good company and a skilful chess-player.

He opened the door himself, a tall, powerful man in his shirt-sleeves, his greying hair in disorder. At the sight of Christer his face lit up with relief.

'It's you, Christer,' he exclaimed. 'Thank God. You're just the person we need. You've no doubt heard about it all.'

Christer said he had and followed him into a dark but very beautiful room filled with oak furniture with green upholstery.

Gretel Strom burst into floods of tears as soon as she caught sight of him.

'Oh, Christer, dear Christer. Isn't it simply *awful*. My poor little Anneli. And the wedding's at five o'clock and what shall we do about all the guests. Where *do* you think she can be?'

Gretel was fifty-five and rather small and plump. Her hair was still fair and her face had also retained some of the doll-like prettiness which in its time had enchanted a good many men in the district. From an intellectual point of view, she was not quite so well equipped.

Christer tried in vain to extract some sensible information from her.

'She's gone. As if swallowed up by the earth, you see. And we, who were to have packed her cases last night and ironed her underclothes and changed the place-lists, that is, Joakim and she were going to do it, you know what it's like, always someone who is coming or isn't coming at the last minute just when everything's ready, but we'll just have to hope that there won't be any more refusals *today* . . .'

Neither of the men reminded her that if it were the bride who refused then there would scarcely be any need for place-lists. Christer declined Edward's offer of a drink.

'When did you last see her?' he asked.

Edward hurried to reply.

'Yesterday at lunch. She had to be at the dressmaker's at twelve o'clock and left just before.'

'Was she just as usual?'

'Yes, she was, wasn't she?' Edward was anxious for confirmation from his wife. 'I pulled her leg and said she was looking awfully pale, but in fact she always is pale. And she sighed and said that she was nervous and it would have been pleasanter with a quieter wedding . . .'

'Edward agreed with her.' Gretel pouted her soft lips. 'And yet neither of them has had nearly as much to do as I have. Anneli insisted on staying on at Petren's office to the end, and in the evenings she was out with Joakim, of course. Nothing against that, of course. One well remembers what it was like when one was a girl oneself, but . . .'

It was characteristic of Edward Strom that he interrupted his wife when she began to digress too far, but showed no impatience or brusqueness, and simply came to her assistance with both tact and gentleness.

'We're both absolutely bowled over. There are lots of preparations which we ought to get on with but in some way it seems meaningless to get started on them . . .'

Christer's blue eyes were thoughtful.

'Had she much money with her?'

For once Gretel produced some exact information. She blew her nose thoroughly and said: 'She had no more than about five shillings, that I know, because she stood out there in the porch and put her raincoat into her white shopping bag, and then she said: "I've only got a few shillings. Are you sure I don't have to *pay* Mrs Andersson?" And I called back that Mrs Andersson – that's our hairdresser – you probably know her, Christer, Helen usually goes to the same one – would be paid for everything when the dressing of the bride was over and you needn't trouble about the dressmaker, because I'll settle up with her, but just get a move on so that you're there on time . . .'

'She hasn't got her bank-book, of course, has she? What's the position there? Did she carry it about with her?'

'No,' replied Edward seriously. 'She keeps it locked up with the rest of the valuables in the house in my little safe. And it's been there since she put in her last salary a few days ago. She's always extremely "careful" when it comes to money.'

His wide mouth spread into an amused smile. But the smile swiftly disappeared. He looked searchingly at Christer.

'You think she's run away of her own free will, don't you? That she's realized that she doesn't want Joakim after all, and she panicked and vamoosed? All I can say is, that it's damned well not like Anneli to do such a thing.'

'I am in full agreement with my respected father-in-law *in spe* . . .'

Joakim Cruse unexpectedly sauntered into the room, mumbled his name to Christer Wick, and threw himself into an armchair.

'*In spe* . . . that means that hitherto you are the only one in my longings and my hopes. Perhaps, oh, perhaps this hope will never materialize.'

Christer looked at him with the calm candour with which he always looked at people. He saw a thin man of middle height with a nervous, finely-drawn face, dressed in a light grey suit of remarkable elegance.

Good God, he's wearing a hand-embroidered waistcoat, thought the Chief Inspector.

And a moment later: Those waistcoat buttons, as true as I am sitting here, are diamonds. Real ones.

26

But Joakim brushed his thin hand over his short hair and went on from Edward's statement.

'I certainly shan't argue against your hypothesis that she's had enough of me and wishes to leave me. But it would all fit in better with the picture I have created of my fiancée's character, if she had chosen to look the bull straight in the eye and personally told me the cruel truth. She is, although she looks like a Princess Lily-of-the-Valley, alarmingly honest, and she would, as far as I can judge, never wish to run away or withdraw from a problem the *back way* . . .'

'And your theory?' said Christer. 'What is it?'

'He's overflowing with theories.' Edward Strom suddenly sounded tired. 'But some of them are slightly over-imaginative.'

Joakim turned a pair of reproachful dark grey eyes towards him.

'I'm not the imaginative one here; that's Dina Richardson,' he said. 'She's the one who says that my lovely fiancée yesterday, at three o'clock, stepped over the threshold of Falkman's flower and vegetable shop, never again to return. Well, if one is to believe that statement, what can one imagine of the sequel? To get to the back door, which is undoubtedly there, she must have forced her way past Fanny Falkman's substantial bulk. And the old girl says "nix". And anyhow . . . if she by some mysterious means got past the old girl and left the shop . . . what next, my dear Watson? After having lived in Skoga for six months I find it quite impossible to believe that anyone could walk down a not inconsiderable stretch of one of the town's so-called main streets without being observed by at least twenty people. And by this time, as we and our poor wedding constitute the one and only subject of conversation for Saturday morning, a report of Anneli's departure ought to have reached our ears by now. *Nota bene:* if she ever made a departure.'

Christer nodded slowly. He had been thinking the same thing.

Gretel Strom stared helplessly at her future son-in-law.

'But . . . she can't very well be *still* in Falkman's place?'

He shrugged carelessly.

'Perhaps she's hidden in the cellar. Or in the attic. If Fanny Falkman hasn't got carnivorous plants in the shop.'

For a bridegroom on the verge of losing his bride, his jargon was remarkably lighthearted. But on the other hand, jargon can be useful, for it covers up a great deal . . .

But Gretel did not like it.

'Ugh,' she exclaimed, and rose so emphatically that the blonde waves on her forehead jumped. 'You're horrible. You'd think this had nothing to do with you at all. Well, we'll just have to see. Now I must phone the butcher and see why the meat hasn't come. Tomorrow is another day, come what may.'

Christer took this as a sign that he should depart and as he considered there was nothing much else to be found at Lake House with its tense and complicated wedding fever, he left and strolled slowly down the road. It was lovely summer weather, the sky light blue and the sunlight brilliant. For a second the thought that it would be nice not to have to wear morning dress brushed his mind, but he hurriedly crushed it, partly because he suspected that his frock coat and the wedding dinner from all points of view, even that of the heat, would be infinitely preferable to the consequences of no wedding being held at all.

As he passed the Richardsons' lilac hedge he heard a low whistle and looked up to see Dina on one of the small balconies of the green-painted house. He went in on to the lawn and exchanged a few words with her. She was dressed in red slacks and a blouse which left her throat and shoulders bare, and although her first words were, 'Don't look at me. I'm in curlers,' he looked again and registered how pretty she was.

She hung over the rail and said: 'Anything new?'

The shining black head moved negatively and so she went on:

'I was right, you see. There *was* something odd about her disappearance. But this is all quite crazy. Will there or won't there be a wedding? And what is more important, will there be a dinner at the hotel with salmon and champagne and fresh strawberries? I'm alone at home and haven't a scrap of food in the house.'

28

It appeared that she was no longer taking the fact that her friend had gone up in smoke so hard. Her brown eyes glinted and she smiled cheerfully. Christer bent his head back at an even sharper angle and smiled back.

'I promise to take you to the hotel for dinner. Whatever happens.'

'Fine. Then there's some point in going on beautifying myself. Long dress?'

'And tails?' Christer achieved a tragi-comical grimace. 'We'll settle for that then. After all, I've brought them all the way here.'

As he was speaking he became conscious that her eyes were seeking something – or someone – behind his back. He brought his head back into a natural position and swung right round.

A young man was leaning against one of the gateposts. His hair was thick and fair and his face pleasant and sunburnt; his white shirt had short sleeves and was open at the neck.

He was just greeting Dina, and the change in his expression as he noticed Christer was remarkable. The frank, childishly blue eyes lost their frankness and he appeared to turn sullen and dispirited. Christer brooded in vain over whether it were he himself who had aroused this antipathy or whether the transformation was something as simple – and as suspect – as fear.

'You know each other, don't you?' called Dina from her balcony. 'Christer Wick, the most written-about and most talked-about man in the town, and Leonard Larsson, adversary, schoolfriend and constant companion of Anneli and myself.'

'We've met,' said Christer. 'But I thought you'd moved from Skoga after your parents died.'

Leonard remained dumb, but Dina provided the information instead.

'He's just finished at the Technical College. And now he's got a job at Joakim's factory. Bit of luck, don't you think? Not to mention a few influential connections.'

There was a slight touch of malice in her voice and the

sunburnt youth made a violent gesture. Christer took his pipe out of his jacket pocket.

'Do they need engineers in a coat factory?'

'Yes.' The reply was brief and surly. 'To modernize and care for the machinery.'

The pause that followed was filled by Dina. She directed at Leonard the great question of the day.

'Have you seen Anneli?'

The explosion which had been on its way for some time now detonated with a bang.

'What the hell do you mean? Why the hell should *I* have seen her when no one else has?'

Christer looked at him with interest.

'Did you meet her yesterday?'

'What the bloody hell has . . . ?'

He stopped, kicked a stone with his white rubber-soled shoe and added in a slightly more controlled fashion: 'No, I've not seen anything of her since Wednesday.'

'You waved at her yesterday,' said Dina helpfully. 'When we walked past and you were in the barber's. That was minutes before she was swallowed up by Falkman's flowers.'

Christer Wick's interest increased.

'If I remember rightly, the back of the barber's shop faces the same yard as the florist's. In other words you were remarkably near the place where the great mystery . . .'

The young engineer stared wildly at Christer. Then he blurted out an inarticulate sound which might have been 'bloody hell' and the next second he had swung round on his heel and was gone.

Christer gaped after him in astonishment, but his astonishment deepened when he turned back towards the balcony.

Dina Richardson's face was deathly white, her lips parted and her fingers were fiercely gripping the narrow wooden rail.

Even if it were depressing to be forced to see it, there was no doubt whatsoever that at that moment she had completely forgotten the very existence of Chief Inspector Wick.

Chapter Four

As the hours of the morning advanced, the otherwise relatively sober and peaceful Skoga became more and more like a boiling witch's cauldron. The wedding between Anneli, daughter of dear Doctor Hammar, and a peculiar outsider alone was a first-class sensation, but the latest developments were undoubtedly even more exciting. People huddled at street corners, women arrived home from their Saturday shopping with thin purses but plenty of news, and the telephones sizzled.

'Hullo, is that you, Lily? I must tell you that I met Karin outside Sandelin's, and she said she'd seen Anneli Hammar with her own eyes yesterday, about one o'clock, and she was coming out of Sebastian Petren's office, and Karin swears she was *crying* . . . What? . . . Yes, exactly. Yes, just fancy if he's mixed up in this too. But that's hardly possible. An old man like him.'

'Hullo . . . Hullo, four-eight-two, please . . . Is that you, Ingrid? Have you *heard*? Yes, and they've sent for Christer Wick from Stockholm, so I can't think what they think . . .'

'Hullo. Yes, Gretel Strom's had a nervous breakdown and they've taken her off to hospital in an ambulance . . .'

'Whatever's going on at the exchange? Are you all asleep? Give me seven-one . . . He stood right by me in the post office and he didn't seem a bit worried. Funny, isn't it?'

'What a bad line. They're listening in on the exchange again, I'm sure . . .'

But the poor telephonists in fact had other things to do. The youngest of them finally collapsed and began to weep over the switchboard. But with or without the telephone lines, the chatter went on . . .

The men came home from work and were annoyed to find no food on the table. But they were soon as equally absorbed in the mystery of Anneli Hammar as their wives were.

'She's run away from that red-haired clot,' they said. 'And she's bloody well right too. A nice girl like her . . .'

The wedding guests formed a section of their own in the loquacious and many-voiced choir. They asked one another, as eagerly, if not more so, what on earth had happened and where had she gone? But there were problems which were both unique and troublesome for those involved.

'Is there any *point* in going to the hairdresser, or do you think I should cancel my appointment?'

'Should I put on morning dress and go off to the church? But if there's not going to be a wedding it'll be damned awkward . . .'

'But they haven't cancelled it . . . we can't very well ring them up . . . that'd be too awful.'

At the hotel the head waiter was swearing like a trooper.

'They'll have to pay for the food they've ordered, whatever happens. But it'd be more helpful if they'd tell me whether to stop the laying up in the banqueting-room and to hell with all the floral arrangements. And the extra staff I've got in. What'll I do with them?'

The guests' and hotel manager's dilemma was partly due to the fact that the bridegroom had not succeeded in getting his own way with his future mother-in-law. Gretel Strom had not in fact been taken to hospital in an ambulance – this was just the kind of picturesque exaggeration for which Skoga gossip was noted – but she had been overcome by an hysterical attack of weeping as soon as Joakim had tried to point out that Anneli would presumably not appear in time for the wedding, so it would be appropriate if they cancelled the whole show. Edward Strom and he finally decided on a compromise. If the bride had shown no sign of life by three o'clock, then both men would sit down at their telephones and inform all those involved.

'But,' said Edward Strom wearily, 'it must be much worse for you than for me. Can you really cope with talking to so many people?'

Joakim's dark eyes looked grim.

'Perhaps it's the only way to shorten the conversations. If people have any consideration at all then perhaps they'll show it to the unhappy and abandoned fiancé. I bet it'll be worse for you . . .'

There was another point on which Gretel Strom refused to budge, and that was at any suggestion that the police should be brought in and an S O S sent out over the radio.

'No,' she sobbed, 'I won't have my Anneli treated like a *criminal* . . . Yes, yes, I *know* they do it for others too, but I couldn't bear to hear one of those breezy announcers read out to millions of listeners that when she disappeared "she was wearing a white cotton dress, carrying a white bag, was depressed and hunched up as she walked", not that she was at all depressed or hunched – how does one behave when one is that, anyhow? – but they always *say* that about them all. No doubt it's a formula they use . . .'

Edward Strom brushed his hand over her wet cheeks and promised not to contact the police. When Gretel was out of earshot, nonetheless, he asked for the police station number and poured out his woes to his friend Superintendent Leo Berggren of the local police.

The latter eventually put down the receiver, wiped his forehead with an immense handkerchief and repeated it all to Christer Wick, who was sitting in the chair on the other side of the cluttered desk.

'Consequently,' he said finally, 'we can't intervene yet. Not officially.'

The last two words were pronounced with special emphasis. Christer looked at the fat and genial Superintendent and smiled.

No, Leo Berggren had never been too keen on official action, and now, his sixtieth birthday looming, was even less so. He would soon be retiring and it was typical of him that he had never bothered to exchange his old title for the glossy new one. It was also typical of him that he should add to his last remark: 'Which end shall we begin?'

'Fanny Falkman's,' said Christer, without hesitating. 'She shuts up shop at three and I thought we'd try then. In the meantime you can tell me one or two things which would be useful to know. What, for instance, do you know about the relationship between Anneli and her grand fiancé?'

'Not much,' grunted Leo. 'He appeared in the town last autumn and all the mothers with unmarried daughters

33

flapped round him and asked him to dinner, and I said to the old lady that it was just as well we had already married off our Martha . . .'

Christer lit his pipe.

'Who was it that nabbed him? Was it Gretel Strom or was it Anneli?'

'That's a difficult one. I should say it was more Edward Strom than Gretel who got the first bite. He and Crusc began to play chess and they obviously got on well together. Then the rest must have happened inside the walls of Lake House, but they announced their engagement in the spring and Martha, who has always been a friend of Anneli's, considers she's both in love and happy . . .'

'And the other actors in the drama? There's an engineer, called Larsson . . .'

'Leonard? Yes, he's a nice boy, clever too. Bit puppyish still, perhaps, and unusually vehement when he's annoyed. He's hung around with Anneli and Dina Richardson since they were small, and I suppose we've often wondered which of the two he'd get stuck on.'

For some reason the Chief Inspector avoided discussing Miss Richardson's faults or virtues. Instead he said: 'It is whispered in the town that yesterday Anneli came out of Sebastian Petren's office with tears in her beautiful eyes . . .'

'Oh? As far as I know she ceased working as secretary for Petren several days ago, but she might have visited him all the same. Though what that fat ass could have done which was worth Anneli weeping over is quite beyond my understanding.'

'Your characterizations are distinguished by their exemplary laconic brevity. What about Fanny Falkman?'

Leo Berggren drummed his short fingers on the desk.

'She possesses, as you know, an overwhelming gift of the gab, and she's not exactly neat and tidy. But all the same, she's probably not as slovenly as she looks. She's worked that business up admirably since her husband's death and she's probably quite well off. She's usually either at the little flat in the shop, or else at her house by the greenhouses down in the summer colony area.'

'That's quite near Lake House, isn't it?'

Christer sounded thoughtful.

'Yes,' admitted Berggren, 'it's not far away. But I can't see how that's going to help us. Anneli disappeared in the shop in Little Street, and that's a long way from the nurseries.'

Christer Wick suddenly rose to his feet.

'Forward march, then,' he said lightly. 'I'm burning with desire to see this florist's shop.'

They walked down the street and turned into Little Street, and everywhere – in the bus queues in the square, in the groups of idle youngsters on the benches by the church, and by the kiosk in front of the hotel – people stopped their shopping and discussions and stared after the short corpulent Superintendent and his tall Stockholm colleague. A quarter of an hour later the whole community knew that the pair in question had visited Fanny Falkman's shop. And the guessing and speculation increased in pace . . .

Inside the long narrow shop it was dim despite the two windows on to the street. Green pot plants climbed with serpent-like arms up the walls, the few flowers left over from Saturday were drooping, and everything smelt fusty and enclosed. In the background was a counter on which stood an old-fashioned till and beside the counter an open door led into the store-room.

When the doorbell tinkled, the owner appeared in this doorway. Her eyes were dark brown and hostile as she placed her hands firmly on her hips.

'And now the police,' she said ill-temperedly, 'I might have known. As if it wasn't enough with the place full of hysterical customers babbling away and asking questions ten wise men couldn't answer, but now I'm going to be charged on top of everything else and dragged into court because I didn't see her ladyship Miss Hammar. Well, I can tell you, if I had that Richardson's snotty young madam in here, it'd be a pleasure to put her across the counter and smack her cheeky backside. Inventions and suppositions, that's all she's got to say for herself, and it's a proper scandal that sensible people listen to someone like that rather than to what grown-up reasonable people have to say . . .'

35

'My dear little Mrs Falkman.' Leo Berggren seemed to be happily unaware that he was several inches shorter than the angry woman in front of him. 'Now don't get excited. We have taken Dina Richardson's word for it, and in addition she's prepared to bet her last penny that at least ten other citizens in this town saw Anneli Hammar go into your shop and they've no objections to testifying, should things get that far . . .'

Fanny Falkman, who recognized the justice of this argument, lost some of her high colour, and retreated three steps.

'What do you want?' she mumbled. 'I've nothing . . .'

'We'd like to look around. And perhaps listen . . . to one or two things.'

And the imperturbable policeman stepped past her out into the store-room.

There their attention was immediately caught by a huge bunch of lilies-of-the-valley on one of the long tables fastened along the walls.

Even Fanny Falkman's expression softened.

'Yes,' she said. 'That's her bridal bouquet. I've just fetched it up from the cellar. I thought . . . in case . . .'

Thoughtfully Christer Wick studied the marvellously scented flowers. The little bells were almost transparently white and every stem curved sadly down towards the ground. As if its burden were too heavy to bear.

> King Lily-of-the-Valley
> of the shady grove,
> King Lily-of-the-Valley,
> white as snow;
> the young king grieves
> for the maiden,
> Princess Lily-of-the-Valley.

Had there not been someone who had mentioned Anneli in connection with Fröding's poem? Or was it his associations running wild?

Mrs Falkman's view of the sad flowers was more realistic.

'They're wilting already, and in this temperature it won't be long before they're completely ruined. And I've known

36

that all along. I told Mr Cruse so, and I told him that lilies-of-the-valley shouldn't be picked until the day they are used. But what was the use? He'd got it into his head that the bouquet was to be done the day before, so that his fiancée could come and look at it. "For if she doesn't approve of it, then we'll have to decide on something else." Just imagine! At this time of year, when it's difficult enough to get hold of the flowers anyhow . . . and at a day's notice . . .'

Christer fingered one of the pale green leaves.

'These aren't wild lilies-of-the-valley, are they, although it's the right time of year for them?'

'Well,' said Fanny, now on her own ground, 'the wild ones are mostly over now. But anyhow, they wouldn't have done for Joakim Cruse. He had to have more expensive ones, of course, finer ones, and much more trouble. It's amazing he didn't ask for orchids. But forced lilies-of-the-valley at this time of year are quite frail enough . . .'

Berggren had had enough of flowers.

'Where were you at the critical time yesterday afternoon, Mrs Falkman?'

The chat about lilies-of-the-valley must have done some good, for she was quite co-operative for a while.

'I only had an errand-girl to help me, because my assistant is on holiday, and that means I can't leave the shop during the day.'

Christer had wandered round the bare and sparsely-furnished room. Now he stopped in one of the corners.

'Does this spiral staircase go down to the cellar?'

'Yes, but you needn't worry. I didn't go down there after two o'clock yesterday. Just as the church clock struck two, I came up with Mr Cruse's lilies-of-the-valley, and then I sat in here and made the bouquet whenever I was free between serving in the shop out there.'

'You sat, you said? Where?'

She pointed at a high three-legged stool by one of the wall-tables and explained that the doctor had said she was to sit as much as possible because of her bad legs.

'But it's never for long, I can tell you.'

Both men glanced at each other. The stool was placed next

to the door leading out into the corridor, and if it were true that she had either sat there or served behind the counter in the shop, then there was no possibility that Anneli Hammar could have gone past her unseen.

Christer climbed down the narrow cellar stairs. Fanny Falkman glared sourly after him, and the glare was changed to a scornful smile when he eventually reappeared with an apologetic shake of his head.

'Well, have you finished snooping round now? I've nothing more to exhibit . . .'

But Leo Berggren did not give up so easily.

'Your flat, then? Have you anything against our taking a look at it?'

Fanny tossed her head angrily. She flung open the door leading into the narrow, dark passage, unlocked a similar door in the wall opposite and made a sweeping gesture with her hand.

'By all means, please look. Spies must do their job properly. One room and one kitchen, both minute, no wardrobe, no larder . . . You'd better take a look under the sofa and in the refrigerator too, and we'll see what you find.'

'Now listen, Mrs Falkman.' Berggren's face had reddened. 'It wouldn't be an unreasonable supposition if I guessed that for a few brief moments yesterday afternoon you went into your flat, perhaps to heat some coffee, perhaps to do something else, which you've forgotten about now. During that time Miss Hammar might have had time to get through the store and go on out . . .'

'I'm still quite all there, thank you kindly, Mr Berggren, and I remember very well what I did, and stand by what I've told you.'

She was so angry that sparks flew from her. She hustled the two men before her out into the passage and when they noticed a W.C. at one end of it, she shouted: 'And I was *not* in the toilet. I don't need to be running in and out all day.'

At the opposite end of the passage was a strip of light. Christer pushed open the low back door and stepped out into the yard. In farewell, he said, quite without irony: 'Thank you, Mrs Falkman. You've been a great help to us.'

At once she seemed ashamed.

'I'm sorry if I've been a bit hasty,' she mumbled. 'But it's not pleasant for me either, being dragged into such goings on.'

'And besides,' she added illogically, 'the shop bell can be heard both in the W.C. and inside the flat, but no bell rang before Mr Cruse arrived. I can swear to that, anyhow.'

The yard was large and cobbled, the grass growing green between the stones. It was completely enclosed by buildings, some beautiful old wooden houses, only one storey high. Two giant maple trees, a bed of potatoes and lettuce, and a tiny cottage painted red completed the ancient and idyllic impression.

But Leo Berggren was not in the mood for idylls.

'Damned female,' he muttered. 'She simply must be lying. Why?'

And he repeated the word with increased heat.

'*Why?*'

Christer lit his black pipe and inhaled the smoke contentedly.

'Either,' he said, 'she is seriously involved in Anneli's disappearance and is beginning to be afraid of the consequences. Or else she's lying for personal reasons and to protect some private secret. Unfortunately it's very common that people become tangled in a web of lies to retain their prestige or avoid revealing their small peculiarities.'

During this little lecture, the Chief Inspector had been carefully observing his surroundings.

'That window over there in the corner, nearest Falkman's — whose is that?'

Leo Berggren seemed somewhat disorientated.

'I'm not really sure where I am. Could it be . . . ? No, of course not, that's the new tobacconist's. And the rest of that building is Jeppson's barber's shop.' He pointed out the different premises carefully. 'Up there between the barber's shop and the fire-wall there's a narrow alley which leads from the yard into River Street. Through the big entrance one comes out into Little Street, as you see. The buildings on the

39

other half of the yard are the back of Sandberg's furniture shop.'

Christer nodded thoughtfully.

'I presume we can't go and search the place?'

'What – Frithiof Sandberg's place?'

Berggren sounded genuinely shocked.

'Well, no. All of them.'

'It would cause a tremendous sensation. And so far, the Anneli Hammar case isn't even an official "case". Besides, it's after four and all the shops are shut.'

'Does anyone live in that scruffy cottage?'

'You've got it, man. Old Mrs Eriksson perhaps has something to report. She's nearly ninety, but there's absolutely nothing wrong with her sight or her inquisitiveness. Ssh, there she is . . .'

Out of the little cottage stepped a white-haired, bent old woman with a thick gnarled stick in her hand. Leaning on this, she limped over to a garden chair and sat down. Her eyes were a pale blue and very lively as they fastened eagerly on to the two figures approaching her.

Leo Berggren bowed respectfully. From the way he bellowed his replies Christer decided that the old woman's hearing was not quite so well preserved as her sight.

'Good afternoon, Mrs Eriksson. How are you? This is Christer Wick, old Judge Wick's boy, if you remember him.'

'Course I remember him.' Her voice was brittle and refined, in remarkable contrast to the policeman's thundering tones. 'You wore a black velvet suit with a lace collar and you had long black curls, and my, oh my, weren't you sweet.'

Christer glanced anxiously at Berggren to see if he were laughing, but Gustava Eriksson fortunately went on to other and, to her, more pressing memories.

'And your father, he was a fine man, he was. I had a daughter who was in service in his parents' home. Yes, dear me, that wasn't yesterday, either . . .'

There was a pause before they could ease her back to the present, but gradually Berggren managed to bring her to the point.

'It's nice and warm here in the sun. Do you always sit out here in the afternoons?'

Yes, she said, if the temperature permitted it, then she did just that.

'So you were sitting here yesterday, then?'

'Yesterday. Oh, yes. It was lovely weather yesterday. I was able to sit out here for several hours then.'

'Several hours at a stretch?'

'Oh, yes. From one o'clock to four. That doesn't happen all that often, that it doesn't. There was only one little shower, but it didn't last more than ten minutes . . .'

Just those ten minutes, thought Christer, when Dina Richardson was standing guard in front of the florist's shop.

'Do you always keep an eye on the time?' he asked a little sceptically.

'Can't miss it with the church clock right next door.' She chuckled, obviously proud of her good sight. 'And it's nice to have something to keep your eye on.'

'Of course, of course. But quite a few people must come and go here. Yesterday, for instance? Wasn't there anything exciting to look at then?'

Suddenly an odd, crafty expression flitted across her wrinkled old bird-like face. But she pressed her lips together and shook her head secretively.

'Oh, yes,' wheedled Berggren, 'there must have been some-one out in the yard.'

'Yes, there was, indeed. The girls from Sandberg's came and had their coffee under the maple, and that skinny Charlie from the barber's made the most of it, of course, and sneaked out to them, though I can't think what such fine girls would see in him . . .'

'No one else? Wasn't Anneli Hammar here? She's slim and very fair . . .'

She interrupted him impatiently.

'You don't have to tell me what the doctor's Anneli looks like. She used to come and see me sometimes, the little angel. But not yesterday, no, not yesterday.'

Christer tried a different tack.

'Can one bring a car into the yard?'

41

'Yes, indeed, the entrance is big enough for most things. Coach and four used to come through in the old days, and they let the horses graze in the yard, while they were in the hotel guzzling and revelling. But now they can't even be bothered to drive in with the goods for the shops, but unload them in the street. No, there's been no car in here since the fair, and then it was old Johansson who wanted to put his old bus in here to keep it safe from those car thieves . . .'

As they were about to leave, Leo Berggren yelled: 'But something happened yesterday, didn't it? What was it? You can't just sit there and not tell us anything about it?'

The shrewd expression returned. Again she pressed her lips together.

'Perhaps it was someone,' persisted Berggren, 'coming out of Fanny Falkman's back door?'

Gustava Eriksson smiled delightedly and said nothing.

'No,' drawled Christer. 'The distance between here and that door is so great that one couldn't possibly expect you to be able to see . . .'

She rose to it unsuspectingly.

'Huh, I saw all right, I did. Just as it stopped raining, it was. He opened the door carefully and then he ran like a frightened rabbit round the corner and out of the entrance. Didn't even stop to say hullo.'

She nodded emphatically to herself and went on with an inimitable mixture of artfulness, injured pride and dignity: 'But it wasn't any good him running like that, however fast. I'd recognize Sebastian Petren, back and front, even if he has, God help us, put on a bit of weight since that summer when these hands of mine changed his nappies. And he can't have been in such a tearing hurry that he didn't even have time to raise his hat to me, me that's years older than he is.'

Chapter Five

AT the moment when the bridal procession in all its pomp should have been leaving the bride's home, the latter was very much more like a house of mourning. Edward Strom, grey in the face with fatigue, heat and worry, had repeated the same phrases so many times down the telephone that they had become completely nightmarish to him. In addition he had had apologetic and dismal conversations with relations who had arrived (Gretel's and Anneli's relations, not his own), and was now trying without much success to console his wife, who was lying on her bed weeping inconsolably and abandonedly. He was being assisted by Dina Richardson and Helena Wick, while Christer stood outside on the veranda twirling a whisky glass in his hand, making an effort to understand the theoretically most unfortunate of the lot of them — the bridegroom who had not become a bridegroom.

Joakim Cruse was drinking more Johnnie Walker than might be considered good for him, even taking his Scottish ancestry into consideration. He was idly lolling in a basket chair and his tone of voice was a trifle frivolous.

'It's a very peculiar situation. Peculiar, and in some ways stimulating. One has become the main character in a drama. A drama which contains sufficient doses of tension and mystery to be indisputably interesting. The worst of it is that in all the classic comedies, the cheated fiancé has to appear as a stupid and egotistical fathead, but who knows, perhaps I've got the qualities needed for the part?'

'Are you quite sure,' said Christer dryly, 'that this is a matter of comedy?'

Joakim's grey eyes darkened a shade.

'What's the difference between comedy and tragedy? In a comic play people set traps for each other and betray one another and the young couple gain their happiness at the expense of the aforementioned fathead; in a tragedy some people die, which really might be considered the only reliable happy ending . . .'

Christer, who realized that this well-dressed, red-haired gentleman had no intention of being serious or of revealing any personal feelings, fell in with his light tone.

'Let's settle for comedy then. But in these rather special circumstances it seems to me that the producer has misfired on two essential points . . .'

'Such as . . . ?'

'First of all the fathead who has been led by the nose by his young protégée and betrothed should be elderly and unpleasant, not a pleasing and sympathetic man in the prime of his life . . .'

Joakim blinked in confusion at this unexpected compliment but contented himself with a mumble: 'Go on.'

'Secondly there should be a gay and innocent youth standing ready in the wings — otherwise there can be neither any amusing developments nor a happy ending. And I was just wondering: where is he?'

The basket chair creaked as Joakim sat up.

'Yes,' he said very quietly, 'I'd like to know that too. But unfortunately I haven't been acquainted with my dear fiancée long enough to lure her secrets out of her . . .'

He sank into a brooding silence but jerked awake as Dina Richardson showed herself in the doorway, and then he added ironically: 'But here is the person who can perhaps help us.'

Dina's brown eyes narrowed.

'Help you with what?' she asked curtly.

'To reveal where my adorable bride has gone . . .'

'To rev . . . ?' She was torn between astonishment, rage and laughter. 'You really are crazy. One moment you refuse to believe me when I tell you she *has* disappeared, and the next you imagine I'm in cahoots with her . . .'

Joakim poured himself out another whisky.

'Who,' he asked rhetorically, 'was Anneli's most intimate friend? Whom did she confide in? Is it possible that she could have made such a decision without consulting her childhood confidante?'

44

Dina drew in her breath.

'You're forgetting something, Mr Cruse,' said Christer coldly. 'We've no evidence at all that she left *voluntarily* . . .'

Joakim made a swift gesture of disbelief and distaste.

'Do you mean that she was . . . kidnapped?'

'I didn't say so.'

Two faces turned towards him in silent anxiety. Dina shivered despite the summer heat.

'I . . . I think I'd better go home for a while.'

Christer rose.

'I'll fetch you at seven.'

Then she smiled a little.

'Fine. But . . . but, Christer. I really don't feel much like getting dolled up in a long dress any longer.'

And although he felt just as she did in relation to dressing up in party clothes, he was nevertheless sorry to see how yesterday's cheerful mood had gone from her.

Before he himself left Lake House, he knocked on the bedroom door and asked Edward Strom if he could have a word with him. Both Edward and Mrs Wick came creeping out, whispering 'Ssh, she's asleep', and took him down to the green drawing-room. He explained that he thought it necessary now to send out an S O S over the wireless and to call in the police, and in this he received his mother's support.

Edward Strom brushed his hand over his greying hair and half-heartedly repeated the arguments which really stemmed from his wife.

'But wouldn't it make the scandal even worse? A grown person surely should have the right to behave as she wishes without putting the police on to her? And Anneli doesn't usually . . .'

'No,' interrupted Helena Wick, 'Anneli isn't usually awkward and foolish. And that's just why the whole thing is so bewildering. Whichever explanation you pick on, it isn't a satisfactory one. Either she was taken away or forced to go underground. Or else she went of her own accord, in which case the reason for doing so is in itself a mystery. And we can't just sit here twiddling our thumbs without even *trying* to find out something about what has happened to her.'

45

Edward Strom looked at her almost gratefully.

'What you say is exactly what I think. But you know what Gretel's like. And I promised her . . .'

He padded backwards and forwards across the room. Now and again he glanced uncertainly towards the bedroom door. Finally he sighed heavily.

'First thing tomorrow,' he mumbled. 'If she hasn't appeared by then . . . Tell Leo Berggren he can get going then.'

On the way home Christer spoke with a certain contempt.

'I'd no idea he was so dependent on Gretel. He appears to be such a self-sufficient man.'

Now it was Helena's turn to sigh.

'It was just the same with her first marriage. Sometimes I wonder whether she simply tames her surroundings by her utter silliness. It's no use trying to be reasonable with Gretel. She doesn't even know what is meant by being reasonable, and she's horribly stubborn. The result is that the only possible way of getting any peace is to pat her on the cheek and let her have her own way . . . And I've noticed that most men will do almost anything to get a bit of peace at home.'

'Quite often,' said Christer. 'I'm glad I'm not married . . . Apropos that, I've asked Dina Richardson out to dinner at the hotel.'

'Dina's a very nice girl,' remarked Helena Wick. 'And she might also be useful in all this.'

Christer laughed.

'And now you'd very much like to know which of those qualities she has to thank for my sudden interest? Dearest Mama, I'm not convinced that I know myself. But one has to find something to do to compensate for the wedding that wasn't.'

Christer and Dina discovered when they arrived at the Skoga hotel that several of the wedding guests had thought along the same lines. A harassed head waiter piloted them to their table in the corner by the window, placed a bowl of daisies between them and informed them in a low voice: 'There's a fearful rush on tonight. And unfortunately not everyone has had the foresight to book a table in advance, as you had, sir. Both the dining-rooms will be full soon, and

46

what shall I do then? To lay up in the banqueting-room would, after all, be a little . . . little . . .'

'Macabre?' suggested Dina helpfully.

She was looking singularly decorative in an off-the-shoulder, egg-shell white dress, against which her own colours seemed twice as warm and alive: the golden brown of her skin, her dark brown page-boy bob, newly done at the hairdresser's, the nut brown in her slanting eyes. She seemed to be in a good mood again and she looked round the long room inquisitively.

'Goodness, what a lot of people. There's Sebastian Petren all alone with rows of glasses in front of him, and over there are the stingy old Anderssons. I'd no idea they ever went to the expense of eating out . . .'

The head waiter lowered his voice even further.

'You see, Miss Richardson, Mr Cruse has given orders that everyone who was invited to the wedding is to have dinner and champagne at his expense, and it has undoubtedly spread round the town.'

'Good Lord,' exclaimed Dina, impressed against her will. 'That's a very grand and generous gesture, I must say. But it suits me down to the ground. I'll get tight on Sir Joakim's champagne with pleasure.'

'Now,' said Christer, when the head waiter had left, 'it is time you accounted for your opinion of Joakim Cruse. It seems to be overwhelmingly negative.'

Dina accepted a light for her cigarette and did not answer for a while.

'I've never met a person before,' she said then, with honesty, 'who made me feel so *divided*. Sometimes he's so charming and nice and pleasant that one wants to hug him and stroke that idiotic jagged hair. And then he's so silly and so irritating that I'd like to scratch him, but at the same time I think it's possible that he can't help it.'

'Why not?'

'Oh, it sounds stupid . . . but . . . but sometimes I have a feeling he's . . . a bit wrong in the head. No, don't ask me in what way, because I don't *know*, and presumably I'm nasty and a bit envious.'

'He's certainly an original person,' agreed Christer. 'It's a pity he wasn't born here in Skoga, for then everyone — yes, you too — would accept him for what he is, but he's considered not only an outsider now, but also an incomprehensible and suspect outsider to boot.'

'You mean,' said Dina, 'that there are people born in Skoga who are in their own way as peculiar but no one notices it. Yes, that's true of course, but the main thing is that they're not *strangers*. They were born here, they've lived here all their lives, and everyone knows about their little escapades and irregularities. But Joakim suddenly appears from no-where with his monocle and his millions and no one knows anything about him except that he grew up in Scotland and he speaks differently . . . and . . . one feels uncertain in his presence because one can never make out what he's thinking about or what he's feeling. He seems to be always making fun of things, and . . . yet . . . Have you ever noticed his eyes? They're not at all superior and cynical . . .'

Christer nodded.

'Forgive me if I'm being indiscreet, but I'd be very glad if you could give me some idea what Anneli thought of her fiancé.'

Her eyes met his. It was as if she were testing him for a moment and had then decided to trust him.

'One thing's certain,' she said, 'and that's that Anneli has never discussed him with me. You see, we have been best friends since the cradle, but Anneli has always been shy and quiet about her inner thoughts, and I'm afraid I've mostly been the one who has done the talking over the years. And I certainly never used to mince words over *my* feelings towards Joakim, but she never bothers to defend him even or tell me I'm wrong. She just smiles a little smile and goes pink and says, "I don't want anyone else, anyhow", and then I'm ashamed of course, as one always is when one's lost one's temper with Anneli, and at the same time I'm so awful I brood over what kind of lover Joakim is and whether he is even allowed to love the innocent Anneli at all . . .'

Christer only just prevented his jaw from dropping.

48

'I thought that girl friends always told each other everything in that line.'

'As you heard at Lake House today, Joakim suffered from the same delusion. Dear boys, you both forget that this concerns *Anneli*. And Anneli is unique.'

And Christer concluded, as so many times before, that it was impossible to understand women. Was Dina's last statement dictated by irony or admiration? Was her attitude to Anneli in reality as divided as her attitude to Joakim? He had been under the impression that she was being completely honest with him, but could he really be certain of that?

The arrival of a waiter, two drinks and hors d'œuvre put an end to both the conversation and these thoughts. Christer discovered that he had skipped lunch, Dina assured him she had not eaten any cooked food for four days, and her appetite confirmed this. As they worked their way through the hotel's famous hors d'œuvre they kept off, as if by mutual agreement, all touchy subjects. They chatted about Dina's job in one of the banks in the town, about the weather and mutual acquaintances. Dina asked after Edwin Bure, and Christer was suddenly overwhelmed with a longing for Puck, a longing which only grew worse as they began to consume the champagne. He described his one-year-old goddaughter with such infatuation that Dina finally asked him: 'Why haven't you married?'

'Perhaps I haven't found the right girl.' He raised his glass. 'And if I may return the question into your court?'

She shrugged her brown shoulders lightly.

'The dismal truth is that there isn't anyone who'll have me.'

Did she sound a trifle bitter? In which case he hardly had time to register it, for at that moment Sebastian Petren cruised straight for their table on his way to the cloakroom.

He was flushed and perspiring and his ample stomach almost rested on the salmon as he leaned forward.

'Funny business, this,' he whispered. 'Never heard anything like it in Skoga before. Damned shame for poor Gretel.'

There was little one could say to this, so Christer Wick asked a question instead.

'How did she seem yesterday? Anneli, I mean . . . Was she upset? Depressed? Sad about anything?'

The reply came as authoritatively as the champagne fumes would permit.

'I didn't see Anneli yesterday.'

'Then,' said Christer calmly, 'I must've got it wrong. I thought she paid a visit to your office round about one o'clock.'

'Certainly not. One o'clock . . . at that . . . at that time I was there myself.'

But the eyes behind the gold-rimmed spectacles suddenly flickered.

Christer went on mercilessly.

'And you didn't run into her a few hours later at Falkman's then?'

'At . . . at Falk . . . ?'

It was horrible to observe that the colour of his face could be other than a reddish blue.

He'll have a stroke, thought Dina.

And Christer took his elbow anxiously. But Sebastian pulled himself free absent-mindedly and wandered on like a sleep-walker towards the exit. Christer sank down into his chair again, half-repentant, half-annoyed.

'It's odd, but one can never carry on a conversation to the end with that man . . .'

Dina stared at him.

'What on earth was all that about? Why were you rambling on about Fanny Falkman? Old Sebastian wasn't there yesterday afternoon, surely?'

Christer decided to be open with her. He told her about his and Leo Berggren's visit to the florist's and about Gustava Eriksson's strange revelation.

Dina at once put her finger on the decisive factor.

'There was only one heavy shower during the whole of yesterday and that was during that brief time I was on guard in Little Street and Anneli was inside the shop. If the old girl is absolutely certain Sebastian crept out of Falkman's just as the rain stopped, that means *he must have been in there all the time*. But Christer, that's crazy.'

At that moment Christer discovered that she was very pretty even when she was not smiling. His desire to discuss the non-existent Anneli ebbed slowly away. In some way he was also successful in chasing away the shadows for her most of the evening. Not until the strawberries were finished and the champagne bottle emptied and he had drunk two cups of weak but drinkable coffee, did he return to the subject quite voluntarily.

'Tell me, Dina, what do *you* think about Anneli's disappearance? Even if she didn't confide her innermost secrets to you, you did know her better than anyone else. Quite apart from Sebastian Petren and Fanny Falkman's protestations and the apparent absurdity of the whole situation. Nothing is quite so absurd that it can't be explained in the end . . . Do you think she simply ran away from the bridegroom and all the rest of it?'

'Ye – s.' She frowned in bewilderment. 'Yes, if I have to put it into words, then that's probably what I do think. It's very unlike Anneli to cause such a stir as this, but perhaps . . . if she'd quite unexpectedly heard something about Joakim which . . . which didn't fit in with her picture of him and her ideal . . . You see, she had an awful lot of ideals and ideas about everything, and she wasn't much of a one for compromising.'

'You think that an ordinary quarrel between them couldn't have caused this behaviour of hers?'

Dina sighed.

'Anneli never quarrels. That's what makes her so trying sometimes. And she never loses her temper. Anyhow, she never has done up to now . . .'

She shook her brown head.

'And anyhow . . . where can she have gone?'

'Is it quite unthinkable that there might be another man involved in some way?'

Dina's eyes darkened. But Christer did not know whether this phenomenon were a result of his last remark or whether it had been caused simply by a visual impression. Anyhow her eyes had been directed at something behind his back. He turned round and found for the second time that day that it was Len Larsson who was stealing her attention and interest.

The young engineer was more correctly dressed now than he had been during the morning, but his fair hair still hung down untidily over his sunburnt forehead and he was obviously finding it difficult to maintain his balance. He raised his hand in a kind of careless salute and grinned cheerfully.

'Oh yes, so here you are, celebrating Anneli's escape, are you? You're dead right to do that. I've been drinking her health too, but I've been drinking it alone. Sometimes it's s . . . safer to be alone . . .'

'Len,' said Dina, anxiously and imploringly.

But he raised his hand again, this time with his forefinger and middle finger secretively crossed, nodded briefly and staggered out into the vestibule.

'Shall we take him home?' said Christer, unselfishly.

But Dina's tone of voice was stiff.

'Men who drink themselves silly can manage without my help.'

And from then on she devoted all her attentions to her companion.

They left shortly after midnight and Dina insisted on going over to the florist's shop and also slipping into the shadowy yard. She pressed her nose against the windows of Fanny Falkman's flat and store-room, and she shivered when she saw something white on the window-table inside.

'Look, Christer, it's . . . it's her bouquet. It's withered already . . .'

And as they stood there in silence and in the unreal summer light of the old yard, they both felt depressed. They peered through the window of the shop in which Anneli had so strangely been obliterated, and they saw nothing but the abandoned and drooping flowers. Reluctantly they left, and without speaking wandered along the sleeping small town streets, past drawn blinds and pots of red geraniums, until they reached the Richardsons' garden and Christer kissed Mr Richardson's daughter on a bench down by the lakeside. And Dina was warm and willing . . . It was not her fault that this romantic farewell hour did not become what Christer Wick had expected of it.

Anneli Hammar's shadow had definitely thrust its way between them.

Christer woke at seven after five hours' restless sleep. His first sensation was a feeling of pleasure and delight at being at home. The second was to wonder what it was that had woken him.

A board creaking? A door being shut?

He rose and went through the living-room and out on to the wide balcony of the upper floor of the house. There was no sound either from his mother's bedroom or from Joakim Cruse's flat below. But it was a beautiful Sunday morning. The surface of Lake Skoga lay absolutely still and velvet smooth in the sunlight, the mountains beyond the north shore shimmered and a few yards away a green-painted rowing-boat was reflected in the brown water. Christer made a swift decision and ten minutes later was sitting, dressed in trousers, shirt and sandals, on the seat of the little boat.

At first he headed straight out on to the water but then he changed his mind and instead turned northwards. The bathing place out by the summer cottages would be as good as anywhere.

He glided a little thoughtfully past the Richardsons' garden and came to the Stroms'. The century-old trees had grown both higher and thicker since Christer's boyhood years, and he was surprised that he could no longer see the actual house from the lake.

And then he stopped the boat so violently that he almost broke the oars.

He half-rose to be able to see better, but the boat responded with such a violent tilt that he thought better of it, and sat down again. He backed with swift short strokes in towards Lake House, all the time with his eyes fixed on the white object at the edge of the lake.

The boat touched shore with a jolt and he jumped up on to one of the large smooth stones forming a boundary between the garden and the water.

There he stood absolutely stock still, not even years of professional training preventing him from feeling shocked and confused.

Forty hours after disappearing into a florist's shop in a completely different part of the town, and fourteen hours after the time when as a happy bride she should have been carrying Joakim's lilies-of-the-valley up the church aisle, Anneli Hammar lay among the stones and grass outside her own home. She was lying on her back, her fair hair loose and framing her pale, sorrowful and beautiful face. Her white cotton dress was crumpled and on the left side, across her breast, it was torn and bloodstained. Beside her on the grass stood a white shopping bag.

But what made the scene so fantastic and nightmarish was not any one of these circumstances. It was the fact that she was lying with her small hands peacefully clasped round a bouquet of lilies-of-the-valley.

And although the sun's warm bright rays fell over the shore, the dead girl and the white bouquet, the lilies-of-the-valley were neither drooping nor withered. On the contrary.

They were strong and straight as if they had been picked a few minutes before; when Christer touched them gently they seemed to be still dew-drenched and they overwhelmed him for a moment with their fresh heavy woodland scent.

Chapter Six

FOR several long-drawn-out seconds Christer's brain seemed to be completely empty and incapable of any kind of activity. When his mind functioned again his thoughts were disorderly and incomplete and fluctuated vaguely from one question to another.

That wound? How had she got it?

A knife perhaps? Presumably straight to the heart? But where *is* the knife in that case?

God, how young she is, and so beautiful. I'd forgotten she was so beautiful . . .

But what on earth do these damned lilies-of-the-valley mean? And how can they be so fresh? Someone must have just put them here . . .

What's the time? Nineteen minutes past seven.

Why didn't she bleed more? There's no blood on the ground.

King Lily-of-the-Valley, white as snow . . . the young king grieves . . . I wish I could stop thinking about all those lilies-of-the-valley.

How long has she been lying here?

She is cold but she isn't stiff.

She's not stiff yet.

This fact at last cured the paralysis which had momentarily befallen him. He straightened up and threw a quick look round. The Richardsons' house was just about as near as Anneli's own home. At both places the news of his discovery was going to cause great grief. Christer did not lack compassion, but just because of this it was important that he should not waste too much time on consolations and condolences. Edward Strom would undoubtedly be helpful, but Gretel . . .

In his imagination he saw Gretel's tears flowing, and he resolutely headed for the neighbouring house. A well-worn path along the lakeside brought him to the oddly-shaped

55

green house. He rang the bell and the sound echoed shrilly through the house.

It must have functioned as an alarm, for Dina almost immediately stumbled out on to one of the small balconies on the upper floor. Her hair was rumpled and she was wearing a chic and revealing nylon nightdress, but her sleepy anger was swiftly transformed into a soft and expectant smile.

'But, Christer, what on earth are you doing up so early?'

Chief Inspector Wick sighed again. There were moments when he hated his profession.

'Can you let me in?' he said seriously. 'I need a phone.'

She opened up for him, now wearing a red dressing-gown over her nightdress, and with a frightened expression on her face.

'What . . . what is it? What's happened?'

'It's Anneli. She's been murdered.'

Christer's experience had taught him that it was more merciful to transmit bad news without long preliminaries and evasions, but this time he was afraid that he had been all too brusque about it. Not that Dina Richardson fainted or screamed or behaved hysterically. She simply stood stock still in the little hall and bit by bit her brown skin lost every drop of blood and colour. Her forehead, her cheeks, even her neck turned grey and lifeless like grey paper. Her eyes were unnaturally black and wide open.

Christer put his arm round her anxiously.

'Dina, darling, come and sit down . . .'

But she shook her head and said tonelessly: 'The telephone is in Daddy's room. You go and phone . . . I'd like to be alone for a moment.'

It took an irritatingly long time before anyone reacted at the telephone exchange, but Leo Berggren was very swiftly woken.

'Leo? It's Christer. I've found Anneli Hammar. Dead . . . Yes . . . Yes, no doubt about it . . . Down by the lake in her own garden . . . Can you contact the doc and the State police? I'll see how many people we can spare in Stockholm.'

He was put through to Stockholm with praiseworthy speed.

Christer gave brief orders and even briefer explanations and then returned to Dina.

She had collected herself surprisingly swiftly and overwhelmed him with questions.

'Christer, how do you know it's murder? Where did you find her? Who do you think did it?'

Without waiting for an answer she added, fortunately: 'If I can be any help at all, please just say so.'

'I'd be grateful,' said Christer, 'if you could go and find Mama and tell her.'

Dina nodded sadly.

'She'll be simply wretched. So will Gretel and Edward and ... and ...'

She fell silent and added hesitantly: 'Joakim lives at your place. Shall I ... do you want me to tell him too?'

'That's not necessary. It'd be better to let him sleep as long as possible ... Talking about that ... Did *you* sleep well last night?'

Her pallor was suddenly exchanged for a blush.

'Ye–es, thank you. I couldn't get to sleep for a while, but then I slept very well.'

'Which room do you sleep in?'

'In the gable room up there.'

She pointed.

'The one with the window facing Lake House, then? Was it open?'

'Ye–es. No–o. That is, I shut it about five o'clock.'

'And what did you hear before that?'

'I ... I didn't hear anything.'

'That's impossible, Dina. If you were lying there finding it hard to go to sleep ...'

She flushed again and he thought, slightly uneasily, of their farewell kisses down on the bench in the garden. Had she seen in them something different and perhaps more than he had?

'... then you must have heard lots of noises. People walking past in the road, footsteps, voices?'

'The road ends at the nurseries,' she said curtly. 'And everyone in the neighbourhood had obviously gone to bed before I did. There were some youngsters making a row right out on the lake round about two o'clock, but that's honestly all I have to offer.'

Why did he not trust her? Was it because of her obvious terror when she had been confronted with the concept of murder? And why the hell had she blushed? True, he had drunk a considerable quantity of champagne the previous evening, but his memory was clear and it told him if anything that he on his part had been disappointed in their last hour together, and anyhow he had not seduced her . . .

Christer Wick walked thoughtfully back to the scene of the murder. He glared at a green bench in passing, and promised himself that he would never again complicate an investigation by flirting with slant-eyed and willing girls while on duty. But he had hardly been on duty last night, or had he?

He stopped suddenly and looked at the bench rather more thoroughly. He even went across and sat down on it. Then he whistled.

From the point or small promontory into the lake on which the garden furniture was placed one had a free view across the neighbouring strip of shore. He remembered now that between kisses he had noticed both the round stones at the water's edge as well as the trim canoe up on the grass. On the other hand what had definitely not been there at half past one was the still white figure on the grass. Well, that only supported his previous observation on the stiffness of the body, but in such a complicated case as this one was grateful for all time checks.

For complicated it was, as Christer Wick and Leo Berggren agreed at a low-voiced conference a short while later. Berggren wiped the sweat from the back of his neck, looked from the wax-like face of the dead girl to the increasingly hot sun and mumbled: 'Hope the doc and the men get a move on. She can't stay here for much longer.'

And after another look at the pathetically lovely figure, with its childishly outspread hair and the lilies-of-the-valley, he added: 'Oh, damn and blast it.'

The police doctor said roughly the same thing, though with even more emphasis, a short while later. Daniel Severin, with his shambling walk, his coarse hands and his rugged

58

grey hair, reminded him of a clumsy, shaggy bear, and at this moment an obviously enraged one.

'To go for such a defenceless kid as Anneli Hammar. If you find out who – drove a knife between her ribs, then I'll guarantee personally to wring his bloody neck.'

The deep bass voice rolled across the still surface of the water. Christer, who had fetched his pipe from the boat, started to fill it.

'Oh, yes. You say it was done with a knife, then?'

Doctor Severin knelt down beside the body and at once his hands were sensitive and gentle.

'I'm not saying anything,' he growled over his shoulder, 'and you know that very well. I'm guessing. Your remarkable police doctor isn't able to do anything but guess at this stage. But I've no prestige to lose, so I can afford to guess a bit.'

'I'm all ears.'

'Well. How does this sound? She's been stabbed with a knife, probably quite a substantial one, shall we say some kind of carving knife? It has penetrated between the third and fourth rib on the left side quite near the breast-bone. That means that in all probability it went straight into the heart.'

'But she hardly bled at all?'

'The heart cavity can fill with blood without there being much external bleeding. I presume, still quite hypothetically, that the weapon was not removed from the wound until she was dead, and then she wouldn't have bled at all, of course.'

Daniel Severin's voice was calm and factual and his homely accents were soothing, but that did not prevent Berggren from saying: 'What a hideous picture you've conjured up. And I presume it wasn't a question of a painless or even especially quick death?'

The sunburnt young constable who had appeared in the background seemed to be feeling sick.

But the doctor said comfortingly: 'There is nothing to show she didn't die a few minutes after the stabbing.'

'And when,' asked Christer, 'are we to presume that this all happened?'

59

Daniel rose cumbrously to his feet and scratched his grey head.

'That's more problematical, you know. Much more problematical. It's darned hot here in the sun, so one can't really rely on the ordinary indications like body temperature and rigor mortis.'

'At the moment,' said Christer, 'I'd be content with clarity on one single point. *Could she have been murdered as long ago as on Friday?*'

'You mean . . . ? Almost two days ago?' Daniel's blue eyes expressed genuine astonishment. 'Good God, no. She's been dead four hours at the very most. The autopsy should give more accurate information. But you'd better get a move on with that particular procedure.'

He made preparations to leave, but then stopped and looked up towards the house.

'Have you . . . ? Has anyone told Gretel?'

And when he heard that Christer was just about to go there, he offered to go with him.

'I'm used,' he said with a tragi-comical grimace, 'to telling people about deaths, though, thank God, not usually of this kind.'

They crossed the shady lawn and approached the white house.

'Funny,' thundered Daniel in the tone of voice he himself considered a whisper, 'that they're not awake yet. But they obviously sleep with their windows shut — an unhealthy and extremely reprehensible habit.'

At that precise moment, however, Edward appeared on the veranda. He was barefooted and dressed in blue striped pyjamas, and at the sight of the two intruders his face broke into an astonished grin.

'Well, I'm damned. Gretel was right after all. She's been saying all the morning that there was someone in the garden, and half-asleep I've been assuring her that it was only Petren coming back from a fishing trip. I could hardly have known . . .'

He stopped suddenly and looked at the two of them.

'But . . . what is it? You look so . . . serious.'

'We've brought serious news,' said Christer. 'It's about Anneli.'

The powerful man in front of them leaned heavily on the veranda table. But he did not try to hurry them. He waited in a silence which was painfully tense.

'She's been . . . murdered.'

He swallowed twice.

'Murdered? Anneli? Our Anneli?'

He sounded shocked, absent-minded. Then suddenly it was as if he had grasped the significance of what he had heard, and he exclaimed with genuine despair: 'Oh, my God! My God. However can I tell Gretel that?'

And like an accompaniment to his words, from somewhere in the house came the sound of his wife's anxious, slightly peevish tones:

'Edward. Edward. Where have you got to?'

It was almost terrible to see his agony.

'I . . . I *can't* do it . . .'

Daniel Severin nodded.

'You stay out here. I'll go in to her.'

And the tall figure of the doctor vanished through the door of the dining-room.

Edward Strom sank trembling into a basket chair and hid his face in his hands. Christer sat in silence on the veranda rail.

After a few minutes Edward straightened up and mumbled: 'Who found her?'

'I did.'

'Where?'

'Down by the lake – here.'

'Here? But how on earth . . . ?'

Christer took it as a good sign that he had begun to ask questions and think. And he in his turn prepared to pose a few questions.

'It's all very involved,' he said slowly, 'and if we're to solve the mystery at all – or the mysteries – we'll need all the help we can get.'

The other man licked his dry lips.

'What . . . ? What do you want to know?'

61

'What lay behind Anneli's disappearance on Friday? Had anything happened that day or during the days before? A quarrel at home? A tiff with Joakim?'

'No, nothing in that line. I can guarantee that. Anneli was happy and lively and joined in with the preparations for the wedding with all her heart.'

He had sounded quite decisive, but suddenly a hesitant glint appeared in his blue eyes, and he reluctantly corrected himself.

'Well, obviously I can't answer for how things were between her and Joakim. I can only confirm that she gave every impression of being perfectly happy.'

'And you haven't seen her at Lake House since Friday?'

'No, of course not. What do you mean?'

'She was found murdered here in your garden,' said Christer grimly.

'How . . . how was it done?'

'Looks like a stab-wound in the chest.'

'That's terrible. I can't believe it. Anneli, who was such a nice, peaceable girl.'

'You were happy to have her as a stepdaughter?'

Edward Strom blinked in vain to stop the tears which were now streaming down.

'I never thought,' he said simply, 'that one could become so attached to anyone who was not one's own child. But of course, it's much worse for Gretel . . .'

He sighed and got up.

'I shall have to . . .'

'Just one more thing. Were you disturbed by any noise in the garden last night?'

'No, not until this morning . . . Though I'm not the one to ask. I sleep like a log and I was utterly exhausted last night after all the upset of the last few days. But Gretel wakes up at the slightest click, so perhaps you'd better talk to her.'

But Christer's compassion got the better of his professional curiosity and he said: 'I'll look in later.'

He was in no hurry to leave the cool veranda however, and in lone meditation he smoked his pipe and stared up at the leafy chestnut trees.

62

He knew that in a few hours he would be up to his neck in the routine work an investigation into murder involved; endless questioning of witnesses, conferences with the men who examined the place and all the others who did the ground work, a confusion of clues and leads, which almost without exception would be worthless or false but which would have to be followed up. So it was therefore all the more important that he should try to fix his initial position and make the essential problems in the case of Anneli Hammar clear to himself.

They seemed to him to be concentrated on two hitherto separate events – Anneli's disappearance in the florist's shop on the Friday afternoon and the appearance of her dead body on the Lake House lawn on the Sunday morning. It was a question of finding the explanation for both these apparently inexplicable factors and thus in a logical way linking them together. In this way some minor riddles, such as the non-existent murder weapon or the constantly recurring lilies-of-the-valley, ought to be solved automatically.

Christer Wick sighed lightly. The distance he had to cover before that attractive solution was attained was from all points of view both long and troublesome. If, in fact, a solution were attainable at all. He had had to learn to accept defeat, but something within him rose to resist defeat in this particular case and here in Skoga. Perhaps he was simply a victim of personal vanity; perhaps he perceived that it would be unpleasant and distasteful that an unsolved murder should occur within his mother's circle of acquaintance.

Fortified by these thoughts he decided that while waiting for the arrival of the State police, he would have a word or two with Lake House's nearest neighbours. He wondered whether it were chance alone that so many of the people involved in the case lived within such short distances of the place where the murder had been committed – Dina Richardson on the other side of the lilac hedge, Joakim Cruse a stone's throw or two away, Sebastian Petren across the road, Fanny Falkman just along the road and Len Larsson apparently in a cottage in the same area . . .

He met Helena Wick just outside the gate and this saved

63

him a fruitless visit to Joakim Cruse. Helena, who had considerately wished to take the unhappy news to him, had found the flat empty and her tenant flown.

'Wherever can he be as early as this?'

'Out on the lake, I expect. That was the way I myself had thought of spending this sunny Sunday morning.'

'You know, I just can't imagine him in a boat, with his elegant waistcoats, and anyhow I doubt very much he would be able to manage a pair of oars.'

She smiled a little, but Christer saw that she had been crying, and he kissed her gently on the cheek.

'It's nice of you to go to Gretel. I thought I'd go and wake Sebastian Petren and see what he's got on his conscience.'

Helena raised her dark eyebrows but she did not press him further, and he went on across the road and into the Petrens' large and well-kept garden. Here were trees, bushes and flowers placed with geometrical precision, and in the middle of it all stood an ugly modern stone house, utterly lacking in charm. Christer smiled at the thought of the elaborate and imaginative wooden mansion which Sebastian had previously shared with his elder sisters, but he wondered what it was that made this successful businessman and local bigwig take refuge in this anxious orderliness. As far as he could make out one did not become rich either in the iron trade or the timber trade by developing pedantic correctness.

It took a long time before the said bigwig reacted to Christer's persistent ringing, and when he did open the outside door he was half-dressed and as angry as a wasp.

'What the hell's going on? It's only just past eight and – what's got into you, boy?'

As the sun was shining into his somewhat bloodshot eyes, he backed into the ugly oak-panelled hall, Christer following closely.

'What's going on? Not very nice things, I'm afraid,' he said. 'We've found Anneli Hammar murdered.'

His mouth fell open like a fish gasping for air.

'Mur . . . murdered. No . . . no–o . . .'

Christer could have sworn that he was scared out of his wits as he added: 'Where did you find her?'

Christer was tempted to reply, 'In Fanny Falkman's shop,' but he controlled himself and told the truth.

'Down by the shore at Lake House. And now we want to know what you've been up to during the night.'

But Sebastian Petren had collected himself after the first shock and replied sharply:

'And what can my activities last night have to do with a murder that happened on Friday?'

'On Friday? Where did you get that idea from?'

'I . . . I . . .' he stammered in confusion. 'I thought . . .'

'No,' said Christer quietly, 'she wasn't killed the day before yesterday, but other remarkable things happened then, and I'm just as interested in them. For instance, your secret exit from Mrs Falkman's.'

'My se . . .' He had assumed the poker-face of many business deals. 'My dear boy, you're mad, and I can't imagine what you're talking about. But I'd be delighted to tell you what I was doing last night. After I arrived home from the hotel at about eleven, I went to bed and slept very well until you came and played merry hell with my doorbell.'

Christer began to feel a certain dislike for all these people who had in all innocence spent the night sleeping 'very well'. The usual questions, heard anything? noticed anything? naturally produced negative replies. At one moment only did it seem as if Petren were on the point of revealing something useful.

'Down by the lakeside, did you say? Some time after three o'clock in the morning? But that's not . . . I was . . .'

He stopped however and went on lamely: 'One would have heard any noise.'

'Yes,' said Christer patiently. 'I'm just going to question the neighbours on this point. If you've nothing else to add then I'll go on to Mrs Falkman.'

A slight twitch of Sebastian's eyelids showed that he was unpleasantly surprised. But he said goodbye without further questions or comments.

Fanny Falkman's house was pleasantly overgrown with creepers and lay between the rows of greenhouses not far away. But either the florist was an early riser and had already shaken the dust of the nurseries from her feet, or else she had been warned not to open her door. Christer rang and knocked in vain, and effectively drawn blinds prevented every attempt to look inside.

He returned to the road which ran from the nurseries to the main road and there, among the daisies, clover and corn-flowers he met Dina walking towards him. She was wearing a wide patterned skirt and a sleeveless lace blouse, and she was overwhelmingly lovely to look at.

' "May I beg of the lovely maiden",' quoted Christer admiringly, ' "where thou goest this lovely day?" '

Her eyes met his and she flushed slightly.

'I . . . I was going to see if Len was up. He lives in that little cottage down there.'

She pointed at a minute cottage down by the lake and Christer, his mind poisoned by suspicions caused by the murder, thought: Another one being warned.

It irritated him that he found it so difficult to know what Dina was feeling. Her feelings for himself, for Joakim Cruse, for the hot-tempered engineer over there in the toy cottage . . .

'He's chosen an original place to live in.'

Christer tramped after the seductively swirling skirt between ankle-high clumps of clover.

'He rents it in the summer for practically nothing from Old Ma Falkman. He was going to move into your mother's flat this autumn when Kim and Anneli moved into their new house.'

He had never heard Anneli's fiancé called Kim before and for some reason he thought the nickname suited him.

'But it's wonderful out here.' Dina was still chatting. 'There're no buildings at all and if you go on northwards, there's nothing but meadows and fields and uninhabited plots and the lake down below.'

The cottage was red and white, with a white flagpole on its roof. It had two windows, both wide open. Dina banged loudly on one of them and called: 'Len, you lazy pig. Get up. We want to talk to you.'

Christer remembered his condition at the hotel and prepared himself both to wait and to cope with yet another early morning police-hater. But Len Larsson surprised him on both counts. Almost at once he stepped out of the low door, dressed much as Christer, in light trousers and white shirt, his short fair hair untidier than ever, but he greeted them calmly and soberly and did not seem to have anything against Christer's presence.

'Is it late then? My watch must have stopped.'

'When did you go to bed?' asked Christer.

'Round about midnight.'

He was completely candid.

'And then?'

'Then? What then . . . ? Well, I slept of course.'

Christer said 'Hmm', but it was to Dina that Len turned and said roughly: 'Don't you believe me, then?'

'Yes. Yes, of course I do. Why shouldn't I?' she replied.

'Yes, why not?' Christer changed the subject.

'You were at the barber's on Friday afternoon. At what time did you leave?'

He looked bewildered then. Not afraid or angry as on the day before, only bewildered.

'I can't possibly remember afterwards like this. Half past two — three . . . round about then.'

'Where did you go afterwards? Back to the factory?'

'No.' He smiled slightly. 'Joakim was in a state about the wedding after all, and couldn't work the day before the wedding day and so he gave me the Friday off too, which was decent of him. I rushed round from one place to another all the afternoon, the barber, the shoemaker, the cleaners, the church — I'd promised to see to the decorations there, and we had an awful job getting silver birch . . .'

He fell silent and then added slightly lamely: 'Hullo. You're here too, are you? Talk of the devil . . .'

Joakim Cruse bowed deliberately. He was an astonishing sight standing there in the clover and almond blossom in the June heat in his tailored elegance and grey and white striped waistcoat and black tie, his monocle in his right eye. To add to it all he was leaning on a slim walking stick with a silver top.

His thin face was deathly tired and serious, but his tone of voice was as ironically bantering as ever.

'Might I possibly join in on the conference? If so many highly-qualified brains get together then the sentence can be considered already pronounced on the poor murderer.'

Len's pupils widened.

'Murderer? What the hell are you talking about?'

It was at that moment that Joakim noticed something just by the cottage wall. He poked at it with the ferrule of his stick, stuck his monocle in even more firmly and bent down.

When he straightened up again, he had in his hand three trampled and half-dead lilies-of-the-valley.

Len Larsson backed away in fright as Joakim accusingly held out the miserable remains of the flowers and mumbled: 'It'd be interesting to know where these came from. I don't suppose you by any chance picked them . . .'

He raised his voice and pronounced the final words of his question with insolent and merciless clarity.

'. . . from Anneli's corpse?'

Chapter Seven

CHRISTER WICK'S eyes were very blue as they in turn looked at the three people involved in this melodramatic performance. He noted Dina's fear and confusion as well as Len's sudden green pallor, and Joakim Cruse's clenched hostility. And as they all seemed to have lost their powers of speech it was in the end he himself who broke the tense silence and turned to the man in grey with his next question.

'Mr Cruse,' he drawled, 'is evidently very well informed. It would be nice to know where *you* got your information from.'

He started and lowered both his hands and his eyes.

'I? Oh, I was just walking along the lakeside. There were police all over the place but they didn't stop me seeing . . . what there was to see.'

His tone of voice was completely flat. He looked absently at the crushed flower-stalks and was about to throw them away when Christer rescued them.

'It was clever of you to notice these lying in all the clover and weeds at your feet.'

Christer Wick sounded both sarcastic and thoughtful at the same time.

'I'd like a few words with you some time. *A few words about lilies-of-the-valley* . . .'

It gave Christer a certain feeling of satisfaction to observe how his nonchalant and unmoved attitude was for one fleeting second disturbed. Before Joakim swung round and retreated through the long grass, a red wave of colour had swept over his forehead and darkened the shade of his hair above it.

'Good heavens!' exclaimed Dina. 'What's the matter with *him*? And what's all this talk about lilies-of-the-valley?'

But Christer at once turned his attention to Len, who was looking as if he would like either to faint or be sick as he stammered out: 'Is it . . . is it true? Is she . . . dead?'

'As dead as a person can be,' said Christer coldly.

'But . . . but that's not possible. She was . . .'

His legs gave way beneath him and he was forced to sit down on the grass. Christer sat down on a log in front of him.

'And why is that impossible?' he asked.

'Because . . . because . . . Good God!'

He thrust his fingers through his unruly hair and groaned. Dina seized him anxiously by the shoulder.

'Len . . . pull your socks up. You don't want to be suspected of murder, do you?'

They both sensed the latent warning in her voice. Len slowly raised his head.

'How did it happen?'

Again Dina forestalled Christer.

'They say she was stabbed in the Lake House garden, down by the lake. Not far away from here. But for the trees in the way over there, we'd be able to see all the police.'

She was speaking swiftly and anxiously, as if she were urgently telling him something of immense importance. He nodded thoughtfully.

'When did it happen? Last night?'

'Last night or this morning some time.'

Christer had let her go on. It was often more profitable to listen to a conversation between the people involved in a murder than to question each one separately. But now, however, he intervened.

'It seems odd to me,' he said quietly, 'that no one has asked the most natural of all questions.'

Two pairs of eyes turned towards him, uncertain, searching.

'Anneli disappeared on Friday. She was not murdered until today. *Where has she been in the meantime?*'

He paused to light his pipe again and then went on.

'But perhaps Len can answer that question.'

'Me? Why the hell should I be able to do that? She didn't confide in me. It wasn't to *me* she was engaged.'

He was hurt and upset and vehement, but although Christer was convinced he was hiding something – perhaps something extremely important – he could not budge him. He stubbornly insisted he had nothing to say about Anneli Hammar or the mystery surrounding her. He had slept all

70

through Saturday night and he'd never even noticed the withered lilies-of-the-valley . . .

Christer suppressed a sigh and went in to inspect the modest little summer cottage. There was a bed in which someone had indubitably slept, a kitchen containing a few strong carving knives, a heap of dishes in the sink and two dirty coffee cups on the kitchen table. The sullen young engineer neither could nor wished to remember why there were two, or when they had been used, or how many knives were usually to be found in the drawer. Christer forbade him to remain in the house, and sent a reluctant Dina to fetch a policeman, who eventually relieved him.

Although there was not really a proper path along the lake shore, he chose this shorter route back to the scene of the murder. He passed the ramshackle jetty and a yellow boat in the reeds, crossed the narrow lane which separated the summer colony area from Lake House and dived straight into a scene of routine and perspiring activity.

It was the State police who had arrived and without a word of complaint about a ruined Sunday they had got down to the careful examination of the body and its surroundings. A zealous photographer who did not recognize the long-legged Stockholm inspector shouted impatiently: 'Push off, you bloody fool. Can't you see the place is cordoned off?'

Inspector Lowe was as usual well brushed, well groomed and well dressed, and his sunburn appeared acquired in southern climes. He grinned affectionately at Christer and remarked: 'Funny weddings you have here in Skoga. Pretty girl, too, by the looks of things. The boys nearly wept when they saw it all. But I gather you've been in on it from the beginning? Perhaps we can find a quiet corner and you can put me in the picture and then we can sketch out some kind of plan of action . . .'

The quiet corner was found in the Wick kitchen, where Christer brewed coffee and talked and Andrew Lowe ate cold beef and brawn and listened with such intensity that he occasionally forgot to transfer the food to his mouth.

'Christ!' he said finally, with considerable emphasis. 'I thought I was pretty blasé about crime and murder and

71

peculiarities, but this beats most cases I've come into contact with. A bride who disappears the day before the wedding and appears two days later as a fresh corpse. A bridal bouquet which withers and reappears in the hands of the corpse. A florist's shop and an angry florist. A fat and secretive timber merchant and an angry and secretive engineer in a summer cottage with two dirty coffee cups inside it and trampled lilies-of-the-valley outside it. A non-existent murder weapon . . .'

'. . . and a fiancé with a striped waistcoat and a monocle, who is completely nuts.'

This last sigh came from Leo Berggren, who, hot and annoyed, had appeared in the doorway. Christer gave him a cup of fortifying coffee and smiled at him.

'Have you been having a get-together with Joakim Cruse?'

'A get-together?' Berggren snapped. 'If only one could at least quarrel with the man. Then he'd at least seem a little more human. But he's impossible to talk to.'

He spread himself a hefty sandwich and went on slightly more calmly.

'At first he appeared down at Lake House. Only about half an hour after we'd found Anneli there, but he was all dressed up in a grey suit and *black* tie, for all that. He just strolled up to the poor kid and stared down at her for a long time, and then he said: "She hasn't changed yet." Quite coldly, just as if he'd been talking about a soufflé or an ice-cream sundae which was about to melt. Well, I had other things to do then, so I left him there, but a while later I had him up on to the veranda, where he drank Edward Strom's whisky – at this time of day – and I tried to interrogate him. But it was like trying to catch an eel with your hands. He wasn't discourteous. Not at all. And yet I've no idea whether he was in bed between three and seven last night, whether he heard anything, or saw anything, whether he's wretched or happy . . . And can you guess what he said when I pointed out that he must have known about the death when he was getting dressed this morning?'

Berggren imitated the cultivated, slightly arrogant voice with astonishing skill.

'I simply felt in the mood for a black tie. It seemed very

appropriate for a bridegroom who had lost his beloved the day before, don't you think, Superintendent Berggren?' Leo glared. 'Superintendent Berggren indeed. The snotty devil.'

Christer and Andrew, who had both seen many ambitious men in the force, looked at this unique policeman. When they were holding a council of war a few minutes later, all ranks were forgotten and it was not the senior man's words which carried the day . . .

When the division of labour was considered round Helena Wick's kitchen table, it was decided that Berggren and Lowe should devote most of their attentions to directing the investigations which were directly connected with the murder. Christer Wick, on the other hand, wished to begin elsewhere.

He wished, as he expressed it, to begin from the beginning. Step by step, he wished to follow Anneli Hammar's tracks during that fateful Friday, to attempt to find an explanation for what had happened in the florist's shop, to reveal where she had been in the intervening twenty-four hours and eventually, perhaps, to reach a solution as to why she had met her death at her own home on that night.

When both the others had gone, he shaved and dressed swiftly. He was both eager and a trifle nervous – as always when he threw himself into an involved and difficult case. Like a hound, Puck had once said, a hound straining to be after its victim. Yes, it was probably true that it was a hunt, but it was a hunt with a human quarry. A murderer was to be surrounded. A dangerous person – or perhaps a desperate and frightened person – who had driven a knife into Anneli's warm and beating heart . . .

He stopped for a minute to look at the portrait of the dead girl which was standing on the book-shelf in the hall. It was a new photograph and did justice to her beauty. But there was – in the droop of her neck or in the expression in her eyes – a touch of melancholy which made him wonder if she really had been completely happy. And his resolution to find out the truth about the mystery of Anneli grew even stronger.

Anyone watching the activities of Chief Inspector Wick during the next few hours, however, would have thought that

73

his methods of working were singularly light-hearted and unsystematic. In fact he simply sauntered round the town, visiting some of his mother's friends, drinking coffee at the lakeside café with two white-haired ladies who had been to morning service, and hungrily absorbing as much Skoga gossip as he could gather on this Sunday morning.

And he found out quite a few things.

That Joakim had murdered his fiancée. On this point several informants, men and women, were in full agreement. The theories fell down when it came to detailing the method, but every possible one was offered, from thirteen bullets from a Browning to a poisoned emerald ring and a swordstick.

That Anneli had been forced by her stuck-up mother to become engaged to her murderer-to-be.

That she really loved Leonard Larsson but that the scheming creature Dina Richardson had maligned him to her, or alternatively her to him, so that it had been broken off.

That she really loved a shoe manufacturer from another town, who was married and had four children, and as she could not have him, poor child, she considered it a matter of indifference whom she married.

That business was bad for Joakim Cruse.

That business was bad for Edward Strom.

That business was bad for Sebastian Petren.

That Joakim was a millionaire five times over. And how had he got these millions? If the police enquired into that now?

That old man Petren was mixed up with the widow Falkman in some murky way. What kind of murky? Well, just murky in a general sort of way. The one white-haired lady had indeed heard from a telephonist ... here she remembered unfortunately that telephonists were sworn to silence and she herself fell silent in the middle of a promising sentence.

That Fanny Falkman was prepared to do anything for money. *Anything*. He should talk to the Petren sisters. *They* knew, all right.

That Anneli Hammar really loved a Frenchman, to whom she wrote long glowing letters.

And she had been completely absent-minded at the hairdresser's on Friday.

'Mrs Andersson said that she hardly answered when she was spoken to and she swept straight past my dryer without even speaking, and that's not a bit like her, for whatever you say, she wasn't stuck-up, and took after her father, not her mother . . .'

And she had come rushing out of Petren's office at about one o'clock on Friday, alternately white, red and green in the face. Regardless of the colour, however, it was an inescapable fact that she had been crying. Crying and blowing her nose.

And *no one* in Skoga of either sex had seen her leave Falkman's shop or had even caught sight of her after she had gone into the building.

And with that Christer was back where he had started. How far all this news he had collected was going to take him would be hazardous to judge. As he had grown up in Skoga, he realized that some of it was hair-raisingly exaggerated or quite false, some half-correct, and some presumably relatively reliable. But how was he to sort the sheep from the goats? To arrange police interrogations for all three thousand inhabitants of the town would not be worth it under any circumstance, for then no one would vouch for a single one of the accusations and observations which otherwise were strewn round so generously.

He paid for the coffee and walked up the steep hill to the police station. There he received a report that the police cars had arrived, together, no doubt, with a swarm of newspaper photographers and crime reporters. Lowe can see to them, he thought smugly, and after a couple of telephone calls, he wriggled past a journalist parked on the steps and headed for Little Street.

He had to wait for a moment outside Falkman's and he stared almost hostilely through the window of the empty shop. He was not going to leave the place until he had extracted its secrets . . .

A thin middle-aged man jumped off a bicycle behind him, puffing and blowing, and Christer realized he was one of the people he had arranged to meet. Mr Linstrom was the owner

of the new tobacconist's on the corner of Little Street and
River Street, and was the florist's nearest neighbour. He had a
window facing their communal yard – all this should mean
that he might have some valuable information of some kind.
He was also terribly willing to be of any assistance, and
unlocked the door, demonstrating and gesticulating with
an officiousness dictated by equal portions of a desire for
sensation and natural fussiness. One had an excellent view
through the huge modern shop-window of the small town
cross-roads, and Christer almost immediately asked his leading question. Had Mr Lindstrom at any time during last
Friday seen Anneli Hammar?

He received a more exact and detailed reply than he had
dared hope for.

'Yes, yes indeed. I haven't lived in Skoga for more than a
few months and don't yet know all the celebrities of the town,
but naturally one notices a beautiful girl like Miss Hammar.
And I especially remember passing her in the street on
Friday. It was out there in River Street and she was wearing a
white dress, one of those tailored things with a wide skirt, and
she was with that dark nice friend of hers – I think her name's
Dina Richardson – and she waved and laughed at someone in
the barber's, and I wondered a little who it could be, for her
fiancé was standing in my shop at the time, and I was going
to . . .'

'Do you mean Mr Cruse was here? In here? While you were
strolling about the street?'

Mr Lindstrom cackled as if Christer had said something
indescribably funny.

'Exactly that, yes. Mr Cruse came in to buy some cigars
and cigarettes, but he paid with a big note and it was one of
those days when every customer has nothing but a note, and
I hadn't enough change so I apologized and nipped out to get
the note changed. I looked at my watch and it was twelve
minutes to three and then I remembered that the banks in
this hole shut at two . . .'

'Can you rely on your watch?'

'I check it every morning with the speaking clock,' said the
tobacconist solemnly, and Christer realized that he had found

one of those rarities, a pedant with a mania for – and a memory for – correct time.

The continuation contained all the promise the beginning had held.

'I thought I might try at the barber's, but it was so crowded that I ran into Lundberg's instead. But not only did I have to wait for a customer to be dealt with but at two fifty-three exactly there was also a dreadful shower which didn't begin to go over for a full five minutes, so I didn't get back until two fifty-eight, but Mr Cruse assured me he was in no hurry, and anyhow it was perhaps just as well for his fine suit that I was away so long, because when he had finally been served it had almost stopped raining.'

'Ten minutes,' said Christer thoughtfully. 'So he was alone in here for ten minutes, from two forty-eight to two fifty-eight. He must have seen his fiancée walking past on her way to Falkman's . . .'

But although this was a lead it was for all intents and purposes one which led nowhere. The tobacconist's shop had but one exit; the long shop inside had no door, only a window facing out on to the yard. And although the window was a low one, Christer's imagination refused to rise to Joakim Cruse, in a hand-embroidered waistcoat and a monocle, crawling through the window right under the nose of the all-seeing Gustava Eriksson. And if one presumed he had quickly slipped out of the door on the corner? Had he, within the passage of ten minutes, had time to get himself up River Street, through the gap by the fire-wall, across the road and into Falkman's place again? In which case why? To speak to Anneli? To frighten her? But he could have done that without all those antics.

And where did Sebastian Petren fit into the picture?

Mr Lindstrom confirmed that he had indeed seen Mr Petren, at about a quarter to three. He had then swung round the corner into Little Street and vanished from sight. The tobacconist had nothing more to report, so Christer moved on to Jeppson's barber shop and his next victim.

But there was little to be found there. Friday afternoons were always hectic, and last Friday had been more hectic than

77

usual, and the barber had had other things to do besides looking out of the window and keeping track of the time. Mr
Larsson had been there, yes indeed. He had sat and waited for
a long time, then he'd had a shave and a haircut and there was
nothing else to tell. The barber's shop also had a window
facing the yard and a back door leading into the little alley.
Len Larsson could have vanished in that direction, but how
had *he* escaped old Gustava?

'That old woman's like the Paramount Weekly,' affirmed
Jeppson. 'She watches over that yard like a hawk. One simply
can't get past her.'

As a result Christer visited Gustava Eriksson for a second
time. In the still Sunday morning they talked of the past and
the present, of children who were dead and grandchildren
who were always so busy, and of the blessed sunshine which
warmed and softened stiff old joints.

It was then that Christer, to his own annoyance, had a
somewhat belated lightning thought.

'Yes,' he said. 'Pity the weather isn't always like this. I don't
think it's rained for four days.'

'Oh yes it has. There was quite a shower the day before
yesterday . . . Didn't last long, that I will say, but it was a real
old downpour while it lasted.'

'And you were sitting out here enjoying yourself. You must
have got very wet.'

'Oh no. I had to hurry indoors, of course. But the sky was
soon clear and blue again, just as before, and I could wipe the
chair and sit out again.'

Christer began to realize that this constantly-mentioned
capricious little shower was a highly remarkable factor in the
events of that Friday. It had driven even this inquisitive old
woman to abandoning her observation post, and meanwhile
anyone could have made their way across the yard to – or
from – the back door of Falkman's.

So far the problem was simpler than it had seemed before.
Now it was a question of getting through the door and finding out what had happened inside.

Christer Wick was convinced that Fanny Falkman was
lying or giving false information. Perhaps unconsciously, as

Gustava Eriksson had, but presumably deliberately. To check on the spot what she had said and to think about it, he had ordered one of the young Skoga constables to acquire a set of Mrs Falkman's keys, and together they thoroughly inspected the empty shop. He put himself alternately in Anneli's and Fanny Falkman's position. He observed that from the shop he could look out on to Little Street without risk of being seen himself, and that the store-room window was so close to the tobacconist's that Joakim could have talked in whispers to his fiancée, had he so wished to. He let his colleague keep on opening and closing the outer door and established that the ringing of the bell certainly could be heard in the cellar, in the lavatory and in the little inner room and kitchen – in the latter only very weakly though, and only if none of the intervening doors was closed. After a dubious look at the now dismally shrivelled lilies-of-the-valley out in the store-room, he finally left the flower shop.

Fanny Falkman was already waiting at the police station, and she was, as he had expected, extremely angry.

'I've never been so insulted in all my life. Fetched and taken to the police station. Whatever next! Disgraced all over the town, that's what I am, and all I say is what *right* have you to do such things? I'm telling you. I've done nothing wrong, and if you look elsewhere you'll find some people whose business you might well look into. But in this town, of course, people in certain circles have to be cherished and protected whatever they get up to.'

Christer had placed himself calmly behind Leo Berggren's desk and set about filling his pipe. One of his men had discreetly set the tape-recorder going. Fanny Falkman glared at the microphone but there was no doubt that this large black-haired woman was a trifle scared in the midst of her rage. And she grew even more worried when yet another visitor was shown into the room.

Sebastian Petren was scarlet in the face, an injured worthy. Christer listened patiently to his rather threatening lecture on his rights as a citizen and the perils of the police overstepping the mark in the course of their duties, but they both realized that the weight of his argument was limited by the fact that the official in front of him was not a local one, but a State policeman. He soon fell silent, glancing nervously at Fanny, and with fumbling fingers, extracting a handkerchief with which he wiped his forehead.

Christer said quite expressionlessly: 'We are investigating a murder.'

Petren exploded immediately.

'What the hell has *that* got to do with *us*?'

'Last Friday, at one o'clock, Anneli was seen coming out of your office in Priest Street. She was crying.' Christer's voice was hard now. 'I want to know the reason for her tears.'

'But . . . but I must protest . . .'

Sebastian looked almost foolish. He fought for breath and then went on more authoritatively.

'She had ceased working as my secretary the Saturday before. Since then she has not set foot in my office. If this is why you have had the insolence to drag me here—'

'You know perfectly well that isn't the only reason. You owe me an answer to another question. Why were you in Falkman's flower shop a couple of hours later? What was it that was so secret that you had to *sneak* out the back way?'

A pair of sharp blue eyes met a pair of bloodshot ones behind gold-rimmed spectacles. It became a lengthy duel. The tape-recorder hummed quietly. Fanny Falkman moved uneasily. Suddenly the silence was broken and Christer received two excited and loud-voiced allies.

Like a tornado, Olivia and Livia Petren thrust aside the unfortunate constable and filled the little room to overflowing.

'My dear constable, don't worry. He sent for us himself.'

'Dear Christer, this really is a terrible business. But so exciting. Just like in one of Agatha Christie's nov . . .'

Both ladies noticed at the same moment the occupant of one of the chairs and said in unison: 'But Sebastian! What are *you* doing here? You *can't* be . . .'

And then they grasped who the red-faced woman at his side was. Olivia waved her stubby hands in the air and cried: 'Oooooooh.'

But Livia Petren turned to Christer Wick. Her lilac-coloured headgear quivered emphatically as she intoned formally as if she were a sibyl: 'I *knew* she would be his downfall. She has entangled him in her web, and I regret to have to inform you, Christer, that our dear little Sebastian for many years...'

She blushed a maidenly blush but continued with a tremble in her voice: '... has been living in *sin* with this person.'

Chapter Eight

THE tumult which then ensued in the office at Skoga police station was quite indescribable and gave rise to many, though diverse, versions at coffee mornings. What appeared to be true was that the Misses Petren and Fanny Falkman expressed their opinions of each other so lengthily and so loudly that the tape-recorder ceased to function, that two constables had to hustle the Petren sisters into the next room, but that the affronted florist had before then managed to pull the lilac hat off Livia's wispy head, that brother Petren, after a vain attempt to use his authority as a businessman and councillor, took refuge in a simulated – or perhaps quite natural – heart-attack and had to be placed on a bunk in one of the cells, and that with strong words Christer Wick expressed his regret for ever having brought these lunatic people together on one spot. There was also the fact, however, that he had every reason to be satisfied with the result.

For when the storm had blown itself out and Christer Wick found himself alone with a much-shaken Mrs Falkman, at last the dam walls burst and she willingly told him everything he wished to know.

She and Sebastian had, as she put it, been living together since the previous summer. She was quite open about it and poured scorn on Livia's remark about 'living in sin'.

'Heavens above, what nonsense. I'm over fifty-three and have been married for twenty-five years and been a widow for three. Sebastian will be sixty in November, and although he's a bachelor, he's quite normal, thank God, and needs a woman. Is it all that strange that it happens to be me? But we realized what tittle-tattle there'd be if it all got out, and to tell the truth that great big man is probably *afraid* of what his harpies of sisters would say and do, and I must say, from what we heard today, it's obvious he has good cause to be so. So we've tried hard to keep it a secret, and he never comes to see me except at night out by the nurseries, and I simply can't *think* how they've managed to snoop it all out, but they're phenomenal when it comes to gossip, and I must . . .'

'On Friday,' said Christer, 'he seems to have visited you at your shop, though?'

'Yes, it was very unusual and terribly stupid of him. But he'd just clinched a big deal and was in a very good mood, and as he was walking past, he saw I was alone and couldn't resist the temptation to come in. I hustled him out into the kitchen straight away . . .'

'And then,' said Christer, 'you shut the door between the flat and the shop and didn't hear the bell when Anneli came in.'

She nodded uncomfortably.

'I thought of shutting it for a few seconds but somehow it turned out to be almost ten minutes.'

'And meanwhile anyone could have come in and robbed the till and gone out again.'

Christer's blue eyes were amused. Fanny Falkman laughed apologetically.

'Sometimes one gets flustered and doesn't notice the time rushing by.'

'So you've no idea what time it was when all this happened, then?'

'All I remember was that it was raining hard when we were out in the kitchen. You could hardly see through the window. Sebastian had no coat with him, so he was forced to stay until the shower was over, but I had to leave him and see to the shop. Mr Cruse appeared in the middle of it all and asked after his fiancée, and a moment later Dina Richardson came, but I said I hadn't seen Miss Hammar, because that was true, *I hadn't*, and I saw no reason why I should tell them what I had been doing, but that Richardson girl became more and more obstinate so I lied and said I'd been sitting in the store-room, for I wanted them to stop asking questions and be off.'

She sighed at the thought of that innocent lie which had brought so much else with it.

'I hardly knew what to do when she began proposing to search my flat. It would have been a fine mess if she'd

83

found Mr Petren in my little kitchen, but fortunately he'd heard their voices and crept out the back way.'

'And it didn't occur to you that you ought to have changed your tune and told the truth when it was obvious that Anneli *had* disappeared and the police had arrived on the scene?'

Her high colour took on a deeper hue.

'Sebastian was terrified about the fuss her disappearance caused and didn't at all want to be dragged into any kind of police questioning and discussion of his private life in public. He belongs to one of the best families in Skoga and he's on the council and on the church council, and naturally he's worried about his reputation . . .'

'I find it hard to believe,' said Christer dryly, 'that his reputation would be damaged if he admitted his relationship with you.'

'But you must do. A man in his position, and at our age, with those sisters and the church elders and all that lot!'

'All I can see is that for paltry and private reasons of your own, you've both hindered and lengthened a police investigation.'

Although it was not the first time he had been confronted with an untruthful and unreliable witness, Christer was considerably annoyed and a little while later he vented his irritation on the now very much subdued Sebastian. The latter, who was obviously more embarrassed than his female partner about their autumnal infatuation, confirmed her account word for word, but he added one item of information which was of interest. It was not about the Friday, on which he swore he had not seen Anneli Hammar either at his office or at Mrs Falkman's, but about the previous night – the night of the murder.

'You see, I didn't go straight home from the hotel. I . . . hmm . . . I went out to Fanny's for a while . . . her house is so near . . .'

He was like an awkward schoolboy unable to look the headmaster straight in the eye. Christer looked at him coldly.

'And so you took a little stroll down by the lake while you were out, did you?'

'Yes, yes, exactly. Naturally I should have told you straightaway this morning, but then I'd have had to explain all this to Fanny . . . and . . . well, you know . . . Anyhow, when I left Fanny, the sun had risen and it was such a lovely morning I went round by the lake. I had my boat tied up quite near Lake House and it's always a good thing to take a look at it . . .'

'What time was that?'

'Half past three. Yes, I'm certain of that, because the church clock struck the half hour and I thought what a good thing it was Sunday morning and one could sleep in . . .'

'Half past three?' said Christer thoughtfully. 'And there was no body lying on the grass?'

'There wasn't a soul there, either living or dead. But down by the shore, a few yards inside the Lake House grounds, there was a white bag . . .'

'Anneli's?'

'I didn't think about it then. It was one of those basket-like things of plastic which every female carries nowadays. Of course I wondered who had put it down there, and in fact I went up to look inside it.'

'Well?'

'It had a white raincoat in it. And on top, wrapped in a damp piece of plastic, was a huge bunch of lilies-of-the-valley.'

'Lilies-of-the . . .'

Christer almost choked. And long after Sebastian Petren had left, he sat on, sunk in his thoughts, drawing lilies-of-the-valley on the Superintendent's notepaper.

When the constable announced Joakim Cruse's arrival, he pushed the piece of paper to one side and leaned back indolently. Joakim also crossed one elegantly-pressed light grey leg over the other and succeeded in appearing comfortable and at his ease in the hard visitor's chair. He smiled ironically.

'The police are certainly astonishingly active,' he said. 'I've already been questioned three times, and on each occasion I've given them the scintillating information that my name is Joakim Perceval Lancelot Cruse, born in Edinburgh, a Swedish citizen and not as yet convicted for a criminal

85

offence. Though it is punishment enough to have to carry such names through one's life.'

'One of your parents must obviously have been familiar with King Arthur's knights . . .'

'My mother. Always my mother. My father's contribution was strictly confined to the money. I'm glad my name isn't Lohengrin.'

'The money is Swedish, then?'

'Well, yes. Some of it is invested abroad, but most of it is in industries here at home. Is that relevant to the murder, or am I in for a charge of embezzlement?'

'It is said in the town that business is not so good for you,' said Christer, counting the diamonds in the grey and white striped waistcoat. He made them eight.

Joakim's thin face looked genuinely amused.

'Oh dear, dear. The people of Skoga don't trust me, is that it? Do you know, I once learnt a jingle which is brilliantly characteristic of Skoga gossip.'

And he declaimed dramatically:

> *'One day I heard a rumour*
> *Which turned me pale with fright,*
> *A man had said another man*
> *Had told him with delight.*
> *But then I heard another man*
> *Who said with virtuous glee*
> *That another man had told him*
> *That it had come from me.'*

It was Christer's turn to smile.

'You mustn't underestimate Skoga's secret information service,' he said. 'It can be horribly well-informed and effective.'

'What else has it to say, then?'

'That Anneli was not in love with you,' replied Christer slowly. 'That she was forced by Gretel Strom to become engaged to you.'

He flushed violently, but whether from anger or for any other reason was impossible to say.

'Forced? That's rather a strong way of putting it.'

He pondered for a second and then went on unusually

86

seriously: 'She confided in me, before she accepted my proposal, that she had been very much in love a number of years ago. "More than I am with you," she said honestly. "But I could not have him, and now it's quite over and done with." I . . . I have no real reason to believe otherwise than that she was in love with me.'

'What happened on the Friday? Did you quarrel?'

Joakim's brief spell of candour was replaced by a mocking superiority.

'My dear Chief Inspector. Two turtle-doves do not quarrel. Especially if they don't even meet one another. We parted on Thursday evening, and then Anneli's only worry was that one of the bridesmaids had said she couldn't come. I have not seen her since then.'

'Be careful with your assertions. You must have seen her when she walked past the tobacconist's on her way to Falkman's.'

The grey eyes glittered.

'I wondered when you would realize that I was in the same building as my so mysteriously obliterated fiancée. The worst of it is that I wasn't even aware of her presence. And I did *not* see her pass – without my monocle, my sight is relatively bad.'

'Oh yes,' said Christer agreeably. 'And last night, between half past three and seven, you were sound asleep in your bed, I suppose?'

He shrugged lightly.

'I was *lying* in my bed. That I should also have slept soundly is perhaps too much to demand. I heard you going to bed round about two. And getting up at about seven, just when I had at last managed to get off to sleep.'

'And how did you *know* . . .?'

'Please don't go on about my black tie, not you too. If a poor devil can't choose his tie according to his mood, then you can blame supernatural manifestations . . . concentrate more on lilies-of-the-valley.'

'You've been expecting that subject to come up, haven't you?'

'Naturally. You made me inquisitive this morning.'

87

'It is I who am inquisitive. Why had you chosen that particular flower for the bridal bouquet?'

'Is it an especially original choice? I should have thought it was the opposite. All girls love lilies-of-the-valley.'

'Had Anneli herself said that she wanted them?'

Joakim hesitated for a fraction of a second.

'No, she hadn't. But I'd found out they were her favourite flowers.'

'Do you know why?'

'Why? Oh, you mean there should be a rational explanation even for one's loves and hates. No, I know only that she was very fond of them. I thought, too, that she was very like them. She was shy and proud and lovely and slightly melancholy, just as they are.'

He took his monocle out of his waistcoat pocket and with its help looked with interest at the inquisitive Chief Inspector.

'What is it exactly you're trying to get at?'

And as if this had been his reply Christer said: 'Why were you uncertain all the same that she would not be pleased with your choice? So uncertain that you thought it safest to show her the bouquet on the day before your wedding . . .'

Joakim shifted uncomfortably, but his tone of voice remained cool and bantering.

'How can one ever be certain of anything when it comes to a woman? One day she's kissing you and turning your head, and the next she runs away from the wedding and all the rest. And the consequence of this inconsequence is that she has finally been murdered.'

Christer rose as a sign that the interrogation was at an end.

'You have summarized the whole in an excellent manner. And you can hardly be ignorant of the direction in which this extreme inconsequence points . . .'

Joakim bowed politely and left. After a glance at the clock, Christer also left. On the stairs he was surrounded by a group of eager journalists, and he promised them a press conference later on in the day.

'Fine. But remember that we go to press before midnight. And it'd look a bit better with *some* kind of statement from the police. The investigation continues, we're following up a clue, have certain suspicions and so on and so on. The public seems to feel safer then.'

He grinned happily at them and surmised that they were quite competent to produce these calming assurances of their own accord.

Strictly speaking, more competent than he was. Was he following up a clue? Had he any definite suspicions? The only thing he could wholeheartedly confirm undoubtedly was that 'the investigation was continuing'. Down by the lake he had a brief conference with Andrew Lowe and the men from the Crime Squad, and was as usual filled with admiration at how swiftly and efficiently they worked. Anneli's body had already been taken away and in the laboratory van both the blood from her dress and the mud from the soles of her shoes were being analysed. Every inch of the grass and the edge of the lake had been searched, relatives and neighbours questioned, and the doctor at headquarters was at that moment equipped and ready to perform the autopsy.

Christer discovered that he was hungry and he received with satisfaction a message from Helena Wick that he should come and have his meal with them at Lake House. This suited him all the better, as he had just been planning a talk with Gretel Strom.

To his surprise he found that Gretel Strom was considerably more in control of herself than she had been the previous day. She sat in her black dress at the table with them and her conversation was as vague and pointless as it always had been. The blue eyes in her soft face were more irresolute and perplexed than desperate, like a child who cannot grasp the extent of the evil inflicted on it.

'Just think, I haven't worn this dress since Aunt Sophie died, and that's two years ago soon, and I was *convinced* I wouldn't be able to get it on, for I've put on quite a lot of weight. It's no good denying it, Edward, because I *have*, but it's not too bad after all. Just as well really, for where would I have got hold of a dressmaker just like that?'

Edward Strom seemed tired and depressed, with little desire to talk, but Gretel flowed indefatigably on.

'And they've run on to the rocks at once. They keep asking and asking questions, so that my head goes round in circles. Whether Anneli used to crease her clothes and whether she wore her hair loose. And I've told them she *never* creased her clothes or dirtied them, not even when she was a little thing, and that there never was such a neat and careful person, and she's worn her hair in a chignon for the last three years now. And they want to know if we've lost any *kitchen knives*. I ask you. But I've been through them all and they're all there, even the blunt ones which won't cut any more. But I must say that woman we have as help in the kitchen, she is impossible about putting everything away in the wrong place, and she's careless in other ways too, not drying the glasses properly, and last night the water was left running in the wash-house all night—'

'But she's a good cook,' put in Edward in an attempt to stem the flow.

But nothing could stop his wife now she had begun to criticize Mrs Hansson, and the rest of the meal consisted of a monologue of complaints on this theme. Christer had to make an effort to retire with her on her own for coffee. Edward looked anxiously and compassionately after them, but Christer firmly closed the door and set about trying to extract some useful information out of this loquacious witness.

'Gretel, dear, try to remember exactly how things were on Friday. Was Anneli really as calm and happy as usual?'

'Yes, she was. She sang away in her bath so much so that I was forced to warn her that if you sing in the morning you'll be weeping by the evening. Then she chatted with the postman. They were in the same form at school and they don't meet very often because she's usually at the office when he comes, and then . . .'

Gretel fell silent suddenly. Her smooth forehead was creased with the unusual effort of thinking carefully about what had happened during the course of a day.

'Then she shut herself up in her room. Fancy that now, I'd forgotten all about *that*. She didn't answer when I called her and she was so long we had to wait; it was hash and fried eggs, and that's something you have to eat straight off the stove, or the fried eggs get . . .'

'A letter?' said Christer thoughtfully. 'Well, perhaps . . .'

He already knew that there had been no unusual letter or note either in Anneli's bag or in the drawers of her desk in her room at Lake House. Gretel did not have much to say about her daughter's correspondence either.

'I think she corresponded quite a bit with Len Larsson, but otherwise I don't know . . . Letters from abroad? No, I don't imagine so, but ask Edward; he's the one who usually takes in the post.'

And when Christer cautiously enquired whether Anneli had had a serious love affair before, astonishingly enough he received the same advice.

'Ask Edward.'

She explained without the slightest bitterness, simply stating it as fact, that Anneli had never confided in her about that sort of thing.

'But she and Edward were terribly close and often sat up in the evenings talking. But I have difficulty in getting to sleep and like to go to bed as early as possible. You've *no* idea, Christer, what a burden it is not to be able to sleep, and I simply can't take sleeping tablets because they ruin my head and my stomach, so there's nothing else for it but . . .'

'Are you sensitive to sounds too, Gretel? Noises of different kinds?'

Christer soon realized that he had never really understood how many noises could fill a sleepless night. And even if some of this could be laid on the doorstep of a martyr's exaggeration, he was left in no doubt about the fact that Gretel Strom slept badly and woke at the least sound, either from out of doors or indoors. So it was all the more remarkable that she had not been disturbed by anything the previous night. A drama involving a carving knife could hardly have taken place in complete silence.

Gretel shook her blonde head in amazement.

'We went to bed terribly late, too,' she said. 'Some time between midnight and one o'clock, and then I sleep worse than ever.'

Edward Strom gradually confirmed all this, and he also put forward the hypothesis that the murder had taken place somewhere else and that the body had been taken to Lake House later on, presumably via the lake. He also admitted that Anneli had been more open with him than with her own mother, but he had not been able to break down the wall of reticence behind which she had ensconced herself.

'Yes, I suppose I sensed that she had some love affair behind her which had been both profound and tragic. Tragic because the man in question seems to have been married.'

'Do you know who he was?'

'No. No one from this place, anyhow.'

'Living in France, perhaps?'

'In France? Why do you say that?'

Edward's tired face showed dismay.

'Oh, it was only some little bird told me something about letters from France in connection with Lake House.'

'Well, I didn't usually inspect her post, but I think I would have noticed that.'

'Do you think she was in love with Joakim?'

'I took it for granted that she was. Anyhow, she was quite indifferent to his money.'

He rose and wandered restlessly round the room. It was horrible in some way to see this powerful man, usually so secure and cheerful, on the verge of a nervous breakdown.

'This is unbearable, Christer. What happened to Anneli? Who hated her so? Where has she been since Friday?'

'I don't know,' said Christer calmly. 'But I'm becoming more and more convinced that she vanished of her own free will. She went into Falkman's shop and found it empty except for Joakim's bridal bouquet. For some reason she decided to leave by the back door. I haven't got any further, but I won't give up until the next step is clear. And the next, and the next . . . *Someone* simply must have seen her.'

He repeated this sentence like a formula in a conspiracy during the following wearisome hours as he personally interrogated numerous witnesses at the police station. They were the people who lived along River Street and Little Street, the people who served in the shops in those streets, and

92

the people who had been customers in the shops or had walked along the streets. Leo Berggren's domain became more and more filled with smoke, but through the clouds of tobacco fumes he at last saw a glimmer of light.

The bringer of light was a young housewife whose flat above number fifteen River Street faced the barber's shop and the narrow alley into the yard. She was just asserting that she had not seen anyone of the female sex even remotely like Anneli Hammar, when suddenly she stopped and exclaimed in astonishment: 'It couldn't be . . . ? Supposing that was . . . ?'

Christer repeated patiently that he was interested in every observation, however insignificant it might seem.

'Well, there was a horrid shower of rain. The water absolutely poured down the window-panes, so one couldn't really see anything *through* them. But I was just going to shut a window which had been standing open, when I saw a figure in a white raincoat and a plastic headscarf rushing across the street. Of course, she *could* have come out of the alley, and of course she looked fatter and bigger than Anneli, but one does in that kind of macintosh, so now I come to think about it . . .'

'Where did she go?' said Christer, almost without breathing.

'Into a car standing by the pavement. I'm pretty certain someone was sitting in the car, because it started straight away. I seem to remember it was a blue car . . .'

It was as simple as that. A shower, which for a few brief moments stopped the inquisitive townspeople from looking through their windows, a raincoat and headscarf – and a car.

From that moment it was as if everything were developing more happily and more quickly.

To start with it was no great labour finding the blue car, for on a bench in the police station waiting-room there already sat the youth whom Gustava Eriksson had described as 'that skinny Charlie from the barber's'. And it was true that he was spotty and gangling and not particularly handsome, but he possessed one quality which at this moment was worth infinitely more than external beauty – he was an expert on car-makes and cars. And when Chief Inspector Wick

93

mentioned that according to information received there had been a blue car parked immediately in front of Jeppson's barber's shop on Friday morning, he at once came to the point.

'Mr Larsson's new Saab. Not bad for the price. Am I sure? Gosh, it stood there right under my nose for nearly an hour, and we chatted a lot about it while I was soaping him. When did he go? I don't know, I'm afraid, but I think he nipped into the toilet after his shave, and a moment later it was pouring, and when I looked out again the car had gone.'

Charlie did not have anything more to tell, but what he had said was enough for Christer to send a man to fetch the owner of the blue Saab. And he thought with a certain bitter relief that it would be pleasant at last to meet him eye to eye in neutral surroundings, without distracting females in the background. He had quite a few questions to put to Len Larsson.

But the young engineer did not arrive alone. At his side trotted Dina Richardson on her spiky heels, and she filled the chilly office with the scent of her powder and perfume and visions of brown shoulders, well-shaped legs and sweeping skirts. She looked at Christer and said disarmingly: "I came with Len in case you were so horrid to him that he needed a defence counsel.'

With difficulty Christer tore his eyes away from her.

'It's not impossible that he might need one,' he mumbled.

Len flared up at once.

'What the hell . . . ? What do you mean exactly? I've nothing . . .'

Christer interrupted him brusquely.

'You've sung that song a little too eagerly at all our previous talks, and I've no great faith in it. One just isn't as unbalanced and erratic as you are if one has a clear conscience.'

'But, Christer!'

It was Dina, leaning forward appealingly. She started back, however, when he turned roughly towards her.

'Do you know what happened last Friday as you stood waiting for Anneli in Little Street? No, but if you ask Len

94

here, he can tell you. Tell you how Anneli hurried out the back way to meet him, as they had arranged, and how he picked her up in his car.'

Dina drew her breath in sharply and stared at the man beside her with her mouth open.

Len's face had turned pale and when he saw Dina's reaction, he exclaimed: 'No, no! It wasn't like that at all. We hadn't arranged it at all. It was sheer chance. She rushed across the street just as I was about to start the car, and it was pouring, so of course I opened the door and said, "Jump in." I'd no idea at all where she'd come from and simply wondered whether I could give her a lift somewhere, and then she said, "Where are you going?" and I told her I was really going to the north side of the lake to fetch the silver birch branches for the church. "I'll come with you," she said, and her voice was so odd that I looked at her quickly, but then she turned quite silent, and we drove through the town and out on to the main road and—'

His sudden pause was so unexpected that the two people listening to him looked up quickly.

'Go on,' whispered Dina. 'Oh, go on.'

And for one dizzy moment Christer wondered if they had reached the solution of the riddle. But Len drove all ten of his fingers through his fair hair with a gesture of exhaustion and cried: 'No one will ever believe me. I've known it all along. I . . .'

'What won't anyone believe? How did the car trip end?'

'How did it end?'

His laugh contained a thread of hysteria. And Dina Richardson and Christer for a moment sensed the same feeling overcoming them as they heard the now all too familiar reply.

'*She vanished*. In the middle of the road, into the forest, Anneli Hammar simply dissolved into smoke, just like that.'

Chapter Nine

HE had prepared them when he had said that no one would be inclined to believe him. Nevertheless he was hurt and angry when he saw their confused scepticism.

'Yes, stare away, both of you. But that's nothing to what I did when I came back, dragging birch branches down to the car, and found it empty and abandoned. And if I hadn't been such an absolute bloody fool, I'd have kept the bit of paper and stuck it under your noses.'

Dina's red nails drummed impatiently on the desk.

'Dear Lord, help us understand what he's prattling about. What piece of paper and why? And how far had you got when she sneaked off? All the way?'

'Wouldn't it be more practical,' suggested Christer, 'if Len told us about one thing at a time? You left River Street and went northwards, and then turned on to the main road? What did you talk about?'

'Nothing.' He was still sullen. 'That is, nothing but the weather and windscreen-wipers. It was hard to see out and I had to concentrate on the driving. She didn't say anything until we swung off the main road again, and then her voice was peculiar again . . .'

Len's own voice was not without its peculiarities as he quoted the words of the dead girl.

' "When we were small and shared secrets with each other, we promised never to betray them to anyone else. Can I still trust you?" I was rather surprised, of course. She'd not exactly shown any tendencies to share her secrets with me since she'd become engaged to Joakim, but I nodded to show that she could, and then she said, "I don't want you to tell anyone about this trip in the car—not today and not at any other time, either." She was terribly serious, but a moment later she laughed, and imitating the exaggerated tones we used to use when we were children, she said, "Swear to me." And I crossed my fingers and swore . . .'

96

He sat sunk in his thoughts for a moment and then added almost threateningly: 'And I don't like breaking promises made to Anneli. Not even now . . .'

Although this stubborn loyalty had delayed the whole investigation alarmingly, Christer found his sympathies for the young engineer increasing.

'And then?'

'Well, we took the road along the north shore of the lake. I was going to get birch branches at several places and at first I stopped at the forester's place. I left Anneli in the car outside his gate and nipped up to the house. He wasn't at home, but his wife took me up to the woodpile and showed me the newly-cut silver birches, and I took them down to the road. All that took about ten minutes. It had stopped raining, and I wasn't surprised Anneli had taken the opportunity to stretch her legs a bit – not until I saw the bit of paper resting against the windscreen in front of my seat. She'd torn a page from a notebook I had lying in the map pocket, and on it she'd written: "Don't come and look for me. I'll get back on my own. Remember you swore not to tell." '

Dina Richardson's brown eyes were for once as good as circular.

'It's absolutely crazy. What in heaven's name can Anneli have had to do in the middle of the forest the day before her wedding?'

'Picking lilies-of-the-valley,' suggested Christer, without conviction.

'Lilies-of-the-valley,' retorted Dina, 'can in fact be found much nearer than that. Besides, why should she want to sneak away so mysteriously from us and from everyone else, if all she wanted to do was to pick flowers? Oh no, my dear friends, there's something very fishy about all this. If I hadn't known Anneli so well, I'd say it was something to do with another man.'

'Did any of us know her particularly well, in fact?' Len turned abruptly to face Dina. 'I've thought and thought, and I've decided she was as inaccessible as . . . the Mona Lisa. At times I kidded myself that she was in love with me, but in between I don't think I even existed for her. And I didn't

97

have her confidence, anyhow. There was quite a bit of talk in the town about her corresponding with a Frenchman . . .'

Dina shook her head briskly.

'I asked her about that straight out about a month ago and I've rarely seen such genuine astonishment as she showed then. And anyhow, where would she have got a Frenchman from without my knowing? When she didn't spend her holidays here by the lake, she and I always went everywhere together.'

'Are there any houses along the north shore of the lake?' asked Christer, thus bringing the conversation back to the empty car on the road.

Now it was Len's turn to shake his head.

'A few families live in the village farther on, and then there is the forester's house. That's all.'

'No summer cottages?'

'The shore is not good enough for that. And the forest above the road is more or less impenetrable. I simply can't understand what got into her.'

Christer looked at him through the smoke from his pipe.

'And you've nothing further to add?'

'I? N . . . no. What could I?'

'Anneli wasn't murdered on Friday,' Christer pointed out offhandedly. 'You could have met her several times since then . . .'

Len clenched his fists. For a moment it looked as if he were about to strike Christer for his insinuations. Dina leaned forward quickly and said: 'Christer, you mustn't be suspicious and nasty to this nice boy. Thank him instead for everything he's revealed, and then shut up shop and come with us for a drink and a sandwich.'

She was very pretty and the invitation was tempting, but Christer had other plans.

He had intended to follow up Anneli Hammar's activities step by step until he reached the tragic end, and he did not feel inclined to give up the trail because it appeared to have come to an end in the middle of a road through the forest.

Naturally it was possible that Len Larsson was lying. On some points it was more than possible. But this possibility did not stop Christer Wick from getting into his Mercedes with Leo Berggren at his side, heading northwards and then turning off the main road. Leo Berggren listened and grunted, and as the road wound its way along the northern shore of the lake they could see for themselves that the land to the left of them was mountainous and forested, without buildings until they reached the forester's house.

They got out of the car and with pleasure breathed in the mild scents of pine-needles and moss in the June evening.

'This is where one should live,' said Christer, pushing open the white wooden gate.

But Berggren begged to differ.

'You'd soon get tired of it. No lovely girls for miles.'

'Hm. How far is it to the town?'

'Two or three miles. Quicker straight across the lake, of course, so you could get yourself a motor-boat. And in the winter you could always skate . . .'

Christer accepted his friend's jibes calmly, and with the same calm accepted the fact that the forester was in town and his wife had nothing to tell him whatsoever.

Had she seen Anneli Hammar last Friday?

No, she hadn't seen anyone else except Mr Larsson.

Had she any idea which way Anneli might have taken?

No, there was nothing here but forest and yet more forest, and if one wasn't used to the terrain one would get lost at once. She had indeed found that out for herself, so she knew what she was talking about. No, it wasn't nice living out here. It was much too isolated and lonely, but thank God for the telephone and the wireless.

Were there any good places for lilies-of-the-valley? No, not really, but there were mushrooms in plenty all over the place in the season, and it was very strange that the people living in Skoga had not really discovered this, but they were probably too comfortable to have the energy to climb such steep slopes.

She agreed somewhat reluctantly to send her husband to the police on Monday morning, and the two men drove on to the village. This proved equally unprofitable and during the journey back Christer was silent and brooding.

Thirteen hours had gone by since they had found Anneli murdered in the Lake House grounds. In thirteen hours he had recklessly severed himself from the activities of the police and the Crime Squad and worked along his own private line: *from* the disappearance in the flower shop *up to* the discovery of the body on the Sunday. At one time it had seemed fairly promising. Now it seemed the opposite, as if all he had accomplished was that he had exchanged one mystery for a second and even more obscure and difficult one. Had he been wrong? Perhaps it would have been better if he had stuck to the routine of a murder case and devoted the day to the investigations on the spot, to alibis and to motives?

He was depressed and absent-minded at the press conference which was arranged shortly afterwards at the hotel. But Inspector Lowe, immaculate as usual, presided with evident elegance and skill. No arrest was actually contemplated at the moment. They were awaiting the results of the autopsy and the analysis of diverse pieces of clothing and knives.

Whose clothes?

Which knives?

'Gentlemen, I'll be able to answer those questions tomorrow. To mention any names at this early stage would be foolish and irresponsible towards people who might well be quite innocent.'

The official conference was followed by a more confidential one at the police station. And the more Christer heard of Lowe's, Berggren's and the Crime Squad men's reports, the more his mood brightened. Not because they had in any way succeeded in solving the problems, but simply because he realized that their highly professional activities had not in any way been disturbed by the fact that their superior officer had neglected to interfere in them.

They had photographed, measured and searched every single inch of the lawn at Lake House. They had questioned every person in the neighbourhood of the place where Anneli had lain, and many, many more. They had gathered slippers, pyjamas, shoes, dresses and suits from a long list of people.

Christer asked the same question as the journalists had:
'Which?'
Leo Berggren handed over a list on which was written:

> *Sebastian Petren*
> *Fanny Falkman*
> *Leonard Larsson*
> *Gretel Strom*
> *Edward Strom*
> *Dina Richardson*
> *Helena Wick*
> *Joakim Cruse*

'We ought to have had your name on the list too,' remarked Lowe lightly. 'But to tell you the truth, we don't expect much from the analyses. We've no evidence whatsoever of how the murderer was dressed – pyjamas, evening dress or bathing trunks. But the doctor said on the phone that the stabbing couldn't have been done without bloodshed, and so I wanted to take this opportunity. Besides, I think it might be useful as a warning shot, so to speak. We've also taken a number of kitchen knives and paper knives of the dagger type which seem to tally with the doctor's description of the weapon used.'

'How did they take it?'

'Sebastian Petren kicked up a fuss at first, and Mr Larsson told us to go to the devil, but all the others were very obliging. Joakim politely apologized for his pyjamas not being clean that day, and Gretel Strom offered outright to *wash* the knives before we borrowed them! And wouldn't we prefer a nicer nightgown; there was one in the linen cupboard; the laundry had come back the other day . . . is she as stupid as she sounds, or is it all put on?'

'Both – plus,' muttered Berggren. 'There's no doubt she's somewhat limited, but she can be quite cunning if necessary, or so my womenfolk tell me.'

'It wouldn't be so bad if she didn't flow on so,' sighed Andrew. 'She babbles on and on about trivial and pointless little details and one hasn't the energy—'

'Pointless little details?' Christer suddenly remembered

101

one. 'Tell me, have you the slightest idea *where* the murder took place?'

'No, none at all. As the ground round her showed not a spot of blood, we presume that Anneli was attacked somewhere else and was then taken to the lakeside after her death. But to find the place where she was murdered is a hopeless proposition. The stabbing could have taken place anywhere, indoors or out of doors, here or miles away . . .'

'But wherever it happened it must have left traces of blood, mustn't it?'

'Yes, as long as they haven't been washed away.'

'Exactly,' said Christer eagerly. 'What did Gretel let out as she was complaining about her slovenly help? "And last night the water was left running in the wash-house all night." The wash-house at Lake House, if I remember rightly, is in the outhouses and is quite a way from the main building. That would explain why Gretel didn't wake up and heard neither cries nor voices.'

Lowe was infected by his excitement.

'The wash-house wasn't locked,' he said. 'And the floor was pretty wet, I know, because we inspected it, but not all that thoroughly so far. I'll send a man . . .'

But Leo Berggren scratched his head in puzzlement.

'In the wash-house? What on earth would the girl be doing in there?'

Christer could offer no answer to that, and he saw that again he had created a new problem instead of solving the old one. He sucked on his pipe and sighed.

'Anything else worth noting?'

'Well, we found Anneli's fingerprints here and there in Len Larsson's kitchen. It's possible they're not recent ones. But they appear to be just as abundant – or even more so – at Dina Richardson's and Joakim Cruse's. We also found some hairpins of the kind used by Anneli on the floor of her fiancé's flat. She *might* have dropped them during a struggle which might have preceded the murder. There were a couple of hairpins left in her hair, which point to her hair-do being disarranged by force. On the other hand it seems to have been a habit of hers to strew hairpins about, as far as I can make out. We found several in her own room, and in the kitchen at Lake House, and we found one stuck in a corner of Larsson's kitchen.'

Christer said 'hmm' and then attentively studied the contents of Anneli's white shopping bag. A white raincoat made of plastic, a comb, a pair of sunglasses, a purse containing four shillings, an empty key-ring and a handkerchief which was crumpled and rolled into a hard ball.

'She had been crying,' he remarked laconically.

He was most interested in the items which were absent; the key or keys which should have been hanging from the little steel ring, and the plastic headscarf. He gazed almost angrily at the lilies-of-the-valley which had now found a refuge in Leo Berggren's drinking glass. The 'corpse-bouquet', as the macabre police jargon had christened it, despite the heat of the sun and the photographer's flashes, was still astonishingly fresh, and the slight but penetrating scent of them followed Christer even after he had said goodnight to his colleagues and gone out into the cool evening air.

'Damned flowers,' he mumbled irritably. 'It's either simply sheer chance that they keep cropping up in connection with this case, or their appearance at the scene of the murder is one of those mystifications which are deliberately meant to lead one astray.'

For the moment he refused to admit the third possibility: that they really *were* in themselves a lead, perhaps an essential one . . .

Although it was almost eleven, Helena Wick was not yet home and he walked determinedly across to Lake House to fetch her. Just because Gretel Strom was egocentric and had been stricken with misfortune, there was no reason why his own mother should be worn out.

To his utter astonishment he found a large gathering of people drinking coffee in the old drawing-room. Gretel was presiding over them, dressed in mourning and talking excitedly, sitting on the sofa, flanked by a rather pale-looking Helena and an even more scarlet than normal Sebastian Petren. The latter had, as had Dina and Len, looked in to offer his condolences and at the same time have his worst

103

curiosity satisfied. Joakim Cruse lay sprawled in an arm-chair with an inscrutable expression on his face. None of them seemed to be taking the slightest notice of the fact that their host had deep lines of fatigue in his broad face.

Christer's arrival seemed to encourage Gretel in her stream of chatter.

'Christer, my dear boy, how has everything *gone* for you? Have you got hold of that terrible murderer yet? And what's all this Len's been telling me about his car and Anneli and where they went? You must *see* that she'd never have gone into that awful forest of her *own* free will. And the day before her wedding as well. She knew just how much there was to do. We had some underclothes to iron and the changing of the place-lists . . .'

For once Edward Strom interrupted her quite brusquely, and Christer wondered how many times during the last two days he had had to endure those place-lists and underclothes.

'They say in town that you and Leo Berggren have been out there. How . . . I mean . . . have you any ideas on what might have happened to her?'

Christer met Len's defiant look and suppressed an impulse to discuss his veracity in public.

'No,' he said honestly. 'But we haven't had much time tonight. One can't start searching through forest land except in daylight.'

'None of this,' said Helena, 'is at all like Anneli. Which-ever way I twist or turn, I can't find an even remotely reason-able explanation.'

'Oh yes,' retorted Joakim ironically, 'I can think of *one* explanation.'

'And what would that be?'

They were all speaking at once. Joakim shrugged his light grey shoulders.

'A romantic tryst with a secret lover.'

And he added half to himself: 'King Lily-of-the-Valley of the shady grove . . .'

'You're crazy,' decreed Dina emphatically. 'Would Anneli have made love to another man with your engagement ring on her finger? Right in the middle of uninhabited forest too!'

104

'Well,' said Sebastian Petren, 'I know those forests are damned desolate. They belong to a very suspect firm in the north that refuses to sell either the land or the timber.'

When Helena Wick suddenly drew her dark eyebrows together and frowned, the family likeness between her and her son was impossible to miss.

'But I've heard it said somewhere, by someone or other, that there's a cottage right up in the forest, perhaps on the other side of the ridge. Though there's no way of getting there from the road below – however, I expect there is from the other side. And I can't think who owns it . . .'

'We'll have to tooth-comb the whole area tomorrow,' Christer said grimly.

He went on rapidly to ask for information about two other details: Anneli's plastic headscarf and the empty key-ring. He received a flood of information from all directions, especially from Gretel.

Anneli never took the key of Lake House with her when she went out. The door was nearly always left open, and if the front door were locked, there was always a key hidden out on the veranda. Well . . . hidden . . . Several expressions revealed that they all could have indicated the hiding place in question without the slightest difficulty.

'But the key-ring, then?'

'Oh that,' said Edward. 'She had the keys to Petren's office. But she had returned them last Saturday. Isn't that so, Sebastian?'

'Yes, yes indeed. She gave them back when she stopped working for us.'

The headscarf was described by them all as a triangular piece of white plastic. It had last been seen by Sebastian, who had noticed it in Anneli's abandoned bag by the lakeside, and had been wrapped round a bunch of wet lilies-of-the-valley. Since then it had vanished without a trace.

Why?

Before there was time for any speculation on this problem, Doctor Severin came blundering into the house and immediately ordered Gretel Strom to bed.

'And tonight you're to take these tablets. No, no protests.'

Daniel Severin's loud voice overwhelmed even Gretel's cries and objections. 'I know all about that. You can't take sleeping tablets, your head feels heavy and it upsets your stomach, but you're going to *have* a headache and a stomach-ache tomorrow. It's more important that you sleep tonight. And Edward can keep you company and take two as well. He looks as if he needs them. Anyone else while I'm at it?'

There was a brief pause. Len was the first – half-embarrassed – to stretch out his hand. And then Joakim, his grey eyes serious and desperate.

'Thanks,' he said, 'I'd be glad to accept the offer. Sleep has been in rather short supply just lately.'

Three hours later Christer bitterly regretted not having followed their example. He was exhausted and yet wide awake. Bits of conversation, thoughts and a succession of shreds of evidence whirled round in his brain. Had he let young Larsson off too easily? And Joakim Cruse? Had he been too generous in divulging some things to those who were involved? Had he perhaps warned the criminal? Frightened him off? In a place like Skoga, however, it was a matter of complete indifference whether one questioned people behind locked doors or shouted one's business from the roof-tops. The result was identical in both cases. Within about twenty minutes every inhabitant of the town would know about everything that had been said, whispered, achieved or planned. Every single inhabitant. The murderer too, then ...

After wondering how on earth the murderer himself had managed to bluff this all-knowing and artful and vigilant town, he finally fell asleep and slept soundly, undisturbed by dreams or gloomy forebodings, until the alarm clock's unbearable jangling told him that it was Monday morning again and another strenuous day's work lay ahead of him.

Up at the police station he was told that the wash-house at Lake House had in all probability been visited during the night of the murder. There was water on the floor and the towels and cloths had still been wet on the Sunday evening.

'We've sent them to be analysed,' said Leo Berggren. 'And it'll perhaps amuse you to hear that Gretel's unfortunate Mrs Hansson swears she hasn't set foot in the wash-house for a week. On Friday and Saturday she was busy cleaning and polishing and cooking the lunch that was to be eaten at Lake House the day after the wedding. And though I don't doubt she's careless, I'm pretty sure she's reliable.'

Christer nodded. He was grateful for every small piece of the puzzle they had managed to get hold of. The connecting pattern could hardly begin to grow until they had acquired a considerable number of such small bits.

And he energetically tackled two more witnesses – or rather had friendly talks with them – who might be able to throw some light on a couple of details in the obscure picture.

The first witness was a young man with freckles and clear blue eyes.

Yes, he was the postman, and he would soon have been working for three years in the district in which Lake House stood. He admitted without evasions that he had been in the same form as Anneli and had always admired her good looks, so he had a special interest in her post.

'Of course, she had a right to correspond with as many men as she wanted to, but she had never done so before she got engaged to that red-haired monocle, and so it was quite natural that I kept my eyes open when quite suddenly fat letters started coming with French stamps on them . . .'

'When did she get the first one?'

'Some time in March, I think. And the other one I delivered some time shortly after Easter – April that'd be.'

'No more?'

'No–oo.' He hesitated. 'Unless that one she was so upset about on Friday morning was from the same address. I'm not certain, because there was no name and address on the back, but I thought I recognized the writing. It was unusually strong and nice to look at . . .'

'So there was a name and address on the back of both the other letters then? What was the name?'

The postman flushed slightly, but he did not attempt to evade the question.

'Matthew Norrgard.'

Christer raised his eyebrows.

'Not a Frenchman, then, to judge from the name?'

107

'No. And the last letter, the one that Anneli herself took on Friday, wasn't even from abroad. I'd have remembered if it had been.'

'She was upset, did you say? How do you know?'

'Oh, she was chatting with me, and joking and fooling around, and then her eye fell on the envelope and she stopped in the middle of a sentence. Then she went bright red in the face and looked, yes, well, unhappy in some way or other . . .'

The pleasant young postman also looked unhappy when Christer finally asked how the rumour that Anneli was corresponding with a Frenchman had spread round the town. He promised faithfully never to reveal any professional secrets to his own fiancée, and he left with determined steps to speak firmly to that loquacious lady.

The next victim in the witness chair was a short muscular man who said briefly that he was the forester and that he had been sent there by his wife. He had nothing to offer at first. At the time when Anneli Hammar had disappeared so mysteriously from Mr Larsson's car outside their house, he had not been at home and he was not particularly imaginative when it came to assisting Christer with suggestions as to where she might have gone. But he knew the land he worked on and when Christer asked about a possible cottage up in the mountain, he answered at once.

'Yes, there's one there, all right, but it's not exactly next door to us, either. At least a mile or so back down the road she must have gone, and then she'd have had to climb the hillside and get over the ridge and make her way down the other side. If you come from the other direction, it's much easier to get there, but the place is mighty isolated, whichever way you look at it, and cost a huge sum to build although it was taken there in prefabricated bits . . .'

The forester had suddenly become quite verbose.

'Well, it's none of my business, but if you're the son-in-law to a company that owns thousands of square miles of virgin forest and have the luck to be able to choose which spot you want, then I'm darned if I can see why you go and settle for such an impossible place.'

'Whose is the cottage?'

108

'It belongs to a shoe manufacturer from Orebro. But it's his wife who has the money, though. And she's a queer one, if ever there was one. Whenever she comes, once in a while, and I meet her, she goes on and on about how romantically magnificent it all is and what a marvellous view they have. View! The place is on the wrong side of the mountain ridge and, darn it all, they can't see anything but the tops of the trees. No, it's not very beautiful except for a few weeks in the year, and that's when the lilies-of-the-valley are in flower. I've never seen anything like . . .'

Christer had responded with a certain excitement to the mention of the shoe manufacturer. According to the Skoga gossip — for which he now had an even greater respect — Anneli was supposed to have been in love with such a man with four children. According to the same source, of course, she was also in love with Len and a Frenchman, and none of this really hung together, but when the forester arrived at the lilies-of-the-valley, Christer was nevertheless convinced that he was on the right track. He almost jerked the glass of lilies-of-the-valley under the man's nose.

'Could these have grown up there?'

The forester nodded at once.

'They're over everywhere else. But up there they're always later and usually in flower right up to midsummer . . .'

As Christer rapidly drove out towards the place a moment later, together with the forester and two other men, he could not explain why he was in such a state of excitement. The odds were ten to one that they would find a desolate and closed-up cottage, which was as unlikely as the flowers on the ground to tell them anything about the murder of a woman in white several miles away. And yet he became more and more impatient. It was a relief to him when the forester indicated a narrow path on the edge of the forest and he could hand over the wheel and exhaust himself climbing up the slow incline of the side of the hill.

It was cool and dark under the tall fir trees, the path stony and rough, but he could not go wrong for there were neither crosspaths nor tracks leading off. As they reached the ridge at the top, panting for breath, they were disappointed to notice

109

that the great trees hid the view over the lake and the town. But the forester could think what he liked about the view, for Christer agreed with the manufacturer's wife and gazed in admiration at the billowing lines of darker and lighter foliage which stretched endlessly away towards the horizon.

And then they saw the opening in the forest for which they had been looking. While in general the trees grew closely in this compact pinewood terrain, down below, in a wide hollow in the mountainside, an unexpected and luxuriant glade of straight birches had grown. The sun was playing in the leaves and he was gripped by his old dream of one day, for a few months, being able to live like this – in the middle of the forest, in among the trees and in absolute stillness.

They were soon down by the low brown cottage. The door was open and after a few knocks the forester stepped inside.

But Christer Wick had eyes for nothing else but the birch grove to the left of the cottage and the extravagant wealth of lilies-of-the-valley in the sun-warmed shade below them. Carefully, to avoid trampling on the shimmering white bells, he pushed his way in. It was as if he were trying to extort from them their secret tidings.

Who was she, this creature, who came to you the day before her wedding and who died with you in her hands? What did she want here? What is the answer to her riddle?

He suddenly tripped over a garden chair which had been knocked over.

He looked round in surprise and with a violent shock discovered the immobile figure hanging by a rope from the branch of a birch tree.

His naked legs dangled jointless in the air. With his shattered eyes and his swollen blue face, the hanging man stood out in hideous contrast to the sunlight and the soughing in the trees and the scent of the flowers . . .

Christer had never seen him before. But he knew instinctively that this was the stranger who would have given him the answers to his questions.

Yesterday. Perhaps last night.

But not now.

Now, irrevocably, it was too late.

King Lily-of-the-Valley
of the shady grove,
King Lily-of-the-Valley,
white as snow;
The young king grieves
for the maiden,
Princess Lily-of-the-Valley.

The king lowers his sorrowing head,
Bows in his yielding grief;
Helmets gleam in the
pale soft light
of summer dusk.

Round the spider's webs of the bier,
From the swinging redolent censer,
A coil of incense hovers,
filling the forest
with gentle fragrance.

From the swaying head of the birch tree,
The cool lullaby of the wind,
Small songs of sorrow sound,
and the forest
swells with grief.

A message soughs through the shady dell,
Royal grief in the whispering leaves,
Spreading throughout
the forest realms
from the city of
lilies-of-the-valley.

Chapter Ten

AFTER Christer had sent the forester and a policeman to Skoga to sound the alarm, he made his first inspection of the cottage and the dead man's possessions. The body had been dressed in nothing but a pair of short cotton shorts, but in one of the small bedrooms he found a light summer suit hung carefully up on a hanger. In the breast pocket was a wallet, and this in turn yielded a passport. The passport portrait was no photographic masterpiece, but the general impression it gave of dark hair, regular features and masculinity was a sympathetic one and in some indefinite way a romantic one, and Christer reflected that it was this kind of good looks which must have attracted Anneli Hammar. The stamps in the passport revealed that the owner of it had spent the last four years abroad, mostly in France. His name was Matthew Norrgard and his profession was stated as 'artist'. As he noted that the bed was unmade and the luggage minimal, he wondered in what connection he had come across the name Norrgard and what kind of artist he had been. A bold and colourful picture above the sofa in the big room solved the problem for him, and despite a somewhat scanty interest in modern painting, he now remembered that Norrgard had roused considerable attention at several exhibitions, both through his talent and his originality.

As far as he could see, however, he had not come up to this cottage to paint the magnificent view. His materials were confined to a couple of pencils and an ordinary sketching block, and on this he had carelessly and skilfully sketched a dozen or so variations of the same motif. This was Anneli in all moods and positions, smiling and sorrowful, walking and sitting and standing, with her hair loose and with her hair fastened in a carefully-brushed knot, and finally, in the last sketch, dated June, a laughing and happy Anneli among great drifts of lilies-of-the-valley . . .

But the sketch-book was profitable from other points of

112

view too. Stuck between the back unused pages Christer found the letter which he had not found in the murdered girl's bag, the letter which the freckled postman had delivered to her on the Friday morning and which for some reason she had returned to the writer.

Anneli,
You didn't reply to my earlier epistles and I'm a fool to try for a third time. But I've suffered so much over these years and I've so longed for you ... Now I am at last free, I want at least to say what I've had no right to say before. I love you. Just as much as before. More than before. And as a concession to the dream which has filled my days and nights, I'm going to the cottage for my first week back in Sweden. Our cottage. I shall be there from Friday onwards. And if you reply this time as well with silence then I know what I have to do.
Matthew

Christer could just see the lily-of-the-valley grove through the window. Out there hung the most important witness in the tragedy round Anneli Hammar, his eyes lifeless and his tongue paralysed. It was to him she had gone on the day before her wedding and it was here she had probably stayed during that day on which a scandalized Skoga had been cheated of the most brilliant wedding of a decade. But what had occurred between these two? What had she told him or decided on or done which had led to such tragic consequences for them both?

And what kind of devilish chance had led Christer to this place and this witness half a day too late? Did it mean that he would never reach the final scene in this baffling drama?

When the Crime Squad men with Lowe in the lead swept into the little yard, they were met by a philosophical pipe-smoking Christer Wick, who informed Andrew Lowe rather strangely that he did not believe in chance, anyhow not when it was of the kind behind which seemed to lie a purpose.

Lowe, however, had other things to do besides listening to speculative lectures. To him it seemed indisputable that Matthew Norrgard had committed suicide and that this in itself was as good as a confession to the murder of Anneli.

Daniel Severin boomed his agreement.

'He put the noose round his neck himself and then kicked away the chair he was standing on. How the hell could anyone else have strung him up there like that without knocking him unconscious first?'

'And he hasn't been struck or otherwise assaulted?'

'Not that I can see. He's horribly blue in the face, and there's been some bleeding in the eyes and the eye-membranes, but those are, so to speak, phenomena which must have occurred in connection with the hanging. But, heaven forbid, I'm no expert on all these horrors . . .'

They had stretched the body out on the ground and it was as if the lilies-of-the-valley, by their purity and beauty, emphasized even more the horror and unnaturalness of what had happened. Daniel estimated that death had occurred between one o'clock and four o'clock in the morning, but he recommended a thorough expert examination for more definite information.

Before leaving Skoga, Lowe had telephoned the shoe manufacturer, and after a drive at record speed Mrs Carlmark soon found herself up at the cottage.

She was a slim, middle-aged woman who chain-smoked long American cigarettes. She was extremely distressed but without comment identified the body in the birch grove and afterwards gave Christer some valuable information about Matthew Norrgard.

'We've known him for, let me see, fifteen years now. He was a wonderful painter, but all the same, I think he was an even greater person. I've simply never been able to understand how he managed to be so loyal and good and kind to that hysterical female he was married to. Yes, I know, one shouldn't speak ill of the dead, but one must be honest sometimes, too, otherwise one would explode, and I *can't* be honest about her without being nasty.'

'What was wrong with her?'

'As far as I know, nothing at all, except that she was excessively spoilt and excessively selfish. But she was always complaining about her weak nerves. And she used them to poison Matthew's very existence. If she didn't get what she wanted, or if he showed the slightest sign of freeing himself and living his own life, she fell ill and became a martyr and produced highly dramatic little suicide attempts. Naturally they never succeeded, but they acted as an incessant moral pressure on Matthew and took away all the weapons from his hands. The last few years were the worst. He fell in love with another woman, desperately, seriously and beyond all reason, and I imagine his feelings were reciprocated, but he didn't even dare mention divorcing his wife, but he—'

'Do you know who the woman was, Mrs Carlmark?'

'No. But at a guess I should say it was a girl from Skoga here. He borrowed this cottage for the summer four years ago – about this time of year, as a matter of fact – to be able to paint undisturbed for a few weeks. We have a canoe down by the lake and he was out in it quite a lot. And . . . well . . . it was some time after that holiday that he confided in me that he was extremely unhappy and that he'd decided to move to France . . .'

'Did his wife go with him?'

'Of course. We didn't hear much from them. But last July Matthew wrote a few lines to say she was dying of cancer and she finally died in March. She was buried down there and a few months went by before Matthew came home. But then . . . then he asked if he could have the cottage and we were of course glad to do that service for him. I hoped . . . I really did hope that he would be able to settle things with this girl from Skoga and at last have a little happiness . . .'

'This girl,' said Christer almost sternly, 'was just about to marry someone else. And now she's been murdered, and he is . . .'

'Murdered? You . . . you don't mean it was Anneli Hammar he was in love with? The girl who disappeared from her wedding and who . . . ? But that's terrible.'

'Tell me, Mrs Carlmark, do you think it possible that Matthew Norrgard could have committed a murder? Under the influence of jealousy, despair, anger, years of suppressed longing?'

She thought honestly about the matter.

'No,' she said. 'Suicide, possibly. But not . . . murder.'

'But,' said Andrew, when she had gone, 'the one presupposes the other. If he hadn't stabbed Anneli with a knife, he wouldn't have had to hang himself later ...'

Christer shook his head doubtfully.

'Have you never heard of two people in love with each other who make a suicide pact?'

'In Verona, perhaps,' retorted Andrew Lowe coldly. 'Not here.'

And then he added with a smile: 'What exactly *do* you want? Beautiful Anneli stabbed by an unknown bandit and gentleman Matthew a suicide? Or both victims of a mysterious Mr X? You must admit my theory is less complicated and more likely. Anneli gets a letter the day before her wedding to say that Matthew is at the cottage. She visits him to tell him that everything is definitely at an end between them. He is wild with jealousy and stops her returning in time for the wedding. When she at last escapes from him, he goes after her and kills her. Then he is overcome with fear and guilty conscience and decides to end it all.'

But Christer thoughtfully studied the dead painter's last sketches. The happy, smiling young woman portrayed among the wealth of lilies-of-the-valley had not been forced to stay there. She had chosen of her own free will ...

And then?

Always this 'then'. But he was getting nearer now. Nearer the moment when the mocking shadow of a girl he was looking for, newly-picked lilies-of-the-valley in her bag, reappeared at her home at Lake House.

Voluntarily or not?

Alone or with someone else?

Alive or dead?

Heavy feet tramped all round him. Cameras clicked. Finds were reported.

The rope round the man's neck was relatively new and had probably been cut at both ends with a not very sharp knife. The rest of the rope was not to be found in the area.

Anneli's fingerprints were all over the cottage. So, quite naturally, were Norrgard's. All the others were old ones.

A proud constable came stumping up with something

white in his hand. Naturally, it was a triangular headscarf of white plastic. It had been stuffed under some bushes about five or six yards from the cottage. But why had it been taken out of the shopping bag and hidden up here?

Why? All too many whys . . .

Christer could not agree with Lowe that the mystery was as good as solved. But he did not interfere when a few hours later at the hotel the inspector imparted his views to an imposing gathering of journalists. He could see the newspapers' black headlines already.

MURDERER TAKES HIS OWN LIFE
JEALOUSY BEHIND BRIDE MURDER

Perhaps they were quite right?

And if they were not, then they would have to issue a denial. If and when someone came up with another solution. Until then he had no objections to a breathing space.

He must have time to sort out all the bits of his puzzle. And to think . . .

But the rest of the day did not present many opportunities for quiet contemplation. A case of arson in a near-by town was reported and Lowe hurriedly left, leaving Christer and Leo Berggren to see to the final investigations into the Anneli Hammar case.

'And,' said Christer to the perspiring Berggren, 'as long as I have no conclusive evidence to the contrary, I intend to start from the fact that Matthew Norrgard was also done away with. We'll start by checking up on what some of our friends were up to last night.'

After fortifying himself with sandwiches and a pint of coffee Christer walked out to Skoga's largest industrial enterprise, Cruse's coat factory. He found Joakim in the director's room and noticed that he filled the place behind the magnificent desk with natural dignity and authority. He was more elegant than ever in a black suit, black tie and a waistcoat of discreet black and white stripes; the diamonds had gone and had been replaced with correct buttons of onyx. He looked at Christer through his monocle and asked inquisitively: 'To what do I owe this honour? Have you a warrant for my arrest in your pocket, or shall we have a confidential chat about Life?'

'The latter sounds very pleasant,' said Christer, pulling out his pipe, 'but I've really come to ask whether you have been sleeping well.'

Joakim's eyebrows rose a fraction of an inch.

'What amazing consideration! Are you always so attentive towards your potential criminals? Yes, thank you, I took the doctor's poisonous tablets and they carried me off to the deepest nirvana.'

'When did you go to sleep?'

'Before half past twelve, I should say. Has something special happened?'

Christer did not reply at once.

'You said yesterday,' he then said slowly, 'something rather odd about king lily-of-the-valley. I want to know what you meant by it?'

He noticed to his surprise that the blow had struck home. The young man in front of him flushed and lost some of his poise.

'I . . . well . . . I'm afraid I didn't mean anything at all. Just a silly passing fancy.'

'Would you be more willing to speak if I tell you that we have found him?'

'Anneli's lover?' Joakim's grey eyes darkened disquietingly. 'Or perhaps I should say Anneli's beloved? One can never be quite certain with that girl.'

'You were jealous of him, weren't you? You didn't believe her when she told you that it was all over and done with?'

The thin hands on the polished desk clenched convulsively. The low cultivated voice also at once betrayed a passionate agitation which was all the more intensive because it was so seldom allowed to penetrate that carefully-controlled exterior.

'I wanted,' he said jerkily, 'her to tell me about him, but she closed up like a clam and would tell me nothing. Not what his name was, nor who he was, nor how much he had meant to her, nothing. But I know that it was him she loved, not me. One single thing I did manage to find out and that was that

118

she associated him in her memory with lilies-of-the-valley. And so I had that idea about the bouquet. At first I had desired her, and wanted to have her at any price, but then suddenly it became desperately important that she married me with her eyes open and of her own free will. The bouquet ... it ... it wasn't only a symbol, but also a kind of test which was to force her to take a stand, in some way to choose between the dream of king lily-of-the-valley and me ... I had no idea ... I couldn't possibly know that she'd react so violently and so ... definitely.'

'You were unlucky,' said Christer slowly. 'Matthew Norrgard had written a letter to her, which she got the same morning, a letter which also demanded that she should make up her mind. Your flowers and all their associations in this way played straight into his hands and she decided to run away – to him.'

Joakim Cruse had risen and walked over to the window. The black back was absolutely immobile. But his voice was strained and thick when he mumbled: 'Do you mind ... leaving me alone for a while. Please.'

Christer left without saying anything. His remaining questions could wait ...

He was confused and thoughtful as he mechanically sought out Len Larsson and asked him for his alibi.

Len's boyish face was still sleepy.

'I took both the pills and then went out like a light. I didn't come to until about ten o'clock and was madly late at the factory. But it was good to get some sleep, I must say.'

Christer met Leo Berggren just outside the building which contained Petren's office. Berggren's report was brief.

'Gretel and Edward Strom took the sleeping tablets in view of each other at about a quarter to twelve and snored away until nine o'clock. Dina Richardson was alone at home and maintains that she slept. But something in my little toe tells me that she's lying. You'd better have a go at her yourself. Fanny Falkman was visited by Sebastian Petren. From half past eleven until six in the morning. The old man has evidently become quite randy in his old age.'

They looked up at the lovesick gentleman's office.

'Let's go on up,' said Christer. 'I seem to remember that I

have a bone to pick with this gentleman. It's not good for the image of the police that it is left unpicked.'

Petren opened the outer door himself. As he complained about the difficulties of finding a new secretary, he piloted them through the dark hall and into a room containing an oak desk and upholstered leather chairs. He conjured brandy, whisky and soda out of a solid cupboard and poured out large drinks for them all, despite the other two men's protests. Then he confirmed, relatively untroubled, that he had spent the night with Fanny. Apparently he found it more natural to discuss such matters over a drink in his private office than at the police station. His clever eyes were slyly screwed up behind the gold-rimmed spectacles and he chuckled good-humouredly.

'There you are. Are you satisfied now I've confessed all my terrible sins and relieved my conscience before the servants of the law?'

'Not entirely satisfied.' Christer's voice was less good-humoured. 'You're still holding back some information. What did Anneli Hammar do at this office last Friday?'

'But she never came here,' said Petren. 'I've told you . . .'

'She was observed by several people as she came out. She was crying.'

Sebastian Petren was almost desperate.

'How in God's name can I persuade you that I'm telling you the truth? *She was not here.* I had a business meeting—'

'A meeting with whom?'

'With wh . . . ? Oh, with Edward Strom. He can confirm that . . .'

'Now this is really getting interesting. The girl's stepfather and her ex-employer have a conversation with her which reduces her to tears. She rushes down the stairs—'

'No, no, no!' cried Petren, scarlet in the face. 'We never even saw her. We didn't exchange a single word with her. If she was here at all, she must have slipped in without our knowing.'

'Wasn't the outer door locked?'

'Yes. Yes, but . . . Listen, Christer. I lied to you about the keys. She did in fact forget to give them back and said on the

Tuesday or the Wednesday that she would bring them up next time she was in this direction again. Then I forgot all about them until yesterday when I discovered the keys lying out in that bowl out on the hall table. They must be Anneli's keys, and she could of course have come any time, although if I was in my room at the time I can't understand why she didn't stick her head round the door and say hullo.'

Leo Berggren had already registered the possibilities that had now arisen.

'She must have stood out in the hall and heard you talking inside. What were you talking about?'

'Nothing that could possibly have worried or hurt her, I assure you. We were discussing a project on a mutual deal in timber. Edward's in the same line, you know . . .'

Sebastian had regained his slightly patronizing attitude, and his poker-face also seemed to have returned. Christer realized that for the moment they would get nothing more out of him. But for the sake of form he asked: 'You didn't happen to mention a third person?'

'For instance?'

'For instance Anneli's fiancé, Joakim Cruse?'

'Not that I can remember.'

Although he did not know what he had to gain by continuing along this line, Christer went straight down to Lake House to get Edward's version of this story.

Rumour of Norrgard's suicide had already reached Lake House and for understandable reasons Edward Strom was extremely interested.

'She had told me roughly all about her great love affair, but she never told me his name. I was given the impression that they'd ceased to communicate completely because for special reasons he was unable to divorce his wife.'

'That's probably correct,' said Christer. 'He doesn't seem to have contacted her until after his wife's death this spring either. Presumably he didn't know that Anneli had in the meantime got engaged to someone else. As she hadn't answered his letters, he was probably still unaware of her engagement and approaching wedding when he arrived in the district last Friday.'

Edward's expression clearly showed his mixed feelings.

'It's all so frightfully tragic and meaningless. But at the same time it's a relief to us that Anneli's murderer has been found – and that he didn't turn out to be someone we personally liked.'

Christer suppressed a sigh and hurriedly changed the subject. What was the position? Hadn't Edward paid a visit to Petren's office last Friday?

Edward looked surprised.

'Last Friday? Was it really then? Yes, it might well have been. Between twelve and one, I should say.'

'Did you meet Anneli?'

'Anneli? No, of course not. I saw her last at lunchtime here at home. Why do you ask?'

Christer gave his reasons for asking: Anneli's tears, Sebastian's confession about the keys. Edward stared sceptically at him.

'Do you mean she . . . that she was standing out in the hall eavesdropping on us both? But, my dear Christer, that's not a bit like Anneli.'

Christer had begun to be heartily sick of this reply. But he let it pass, and went on unmoved: 'What did you talk about?'

'Business matters mostly. That's why I was there.'

'What kind of business?'

A broad smile lit up Edward's features for a second.

'Do you want me to initiate the police into our dubious transactions? It was a matter of the purchase and sale of forest lands, and should Anneli have heard anything we said, she wouldn't have understood a jot of it.'

'Did you discuss anything else? Any other person?'

There was a sudden glint in the blue eyes.

'Joakim was certainly mentioned. He was pleased to be able to put some money into our enterprise. But we didn't say anything disparaging about him though.'

Christer's thoughts fluttered hither and thither.

'Had Anneli any money of her own?'

'Nothing much. A thousand or so.'

'And who inherits it? Gretel?'

'Yes. I never adopted the girl. But you can rest assured. Gretel has no need of the money.'

The joke was a little strained.

'I'm sorry,' said Christer. 'That was stupid and clumsy of me.'

Fortunately they were then interrupted by Gretel, who came rushing in, bubbling over with fussy eagerness.

'Someone rang to say that that horrible autopsy is over and done with and we can bury our poor Anneli whenever we wish to. And do you know, Edward, I think it'd be best if we had the funeral as soon as possible. I mean, we've got to go through with it, haven't we, and it'll be just as horrible whenever it is, and at least we've got the house all clean this week and masses of things cooked and . . . yes, yes, Mrs Hansson, I'm *just* coming . . .'

The room was very quiet when she had gone. The two men's eyes met.

'You love her, don't you?'

'Yes,' said Edward simply. 'And so did Anneli. She's . . . she's basically better than she appears. And she needs someone to look after her . . .'

Christer rose and said enviously: 'Anyhow, she doesn't seem to have suffered from Daniel's sleeping tablets. I wish we were half as energetic as she is.'

'It was good for her to sleep the night through. But they must have been pretty strong ones. My head still feels rather heavy.'

He went out on to the steps with Christer. And there he mumbled anxiously: 'Christer . . . It . . . was suicide, wasn't it?'

Unfortunately Christer was not in a position to relieve him of his anxiety. He suspected more than ever that Matthew Norrgard was not the man they were looking for, but instead was yet another victim of that person. The fact of his death occurring rather too conveniently, the plastic headscarf, the cut-off rope, the happy woman in the last sketch in the block – there were far too many details which did not fit. When he returned to the police station after a hasty meal, he could no longer contain his impatience and rang through to the doctor

123

who had performed the autopsy. When they at last got hold of him he seemed reluctant to come to the telephone.

He grumbled lengthily about yet another corpse just when he had completed the report on the first autopsy.

'I'd planned to go back to Stockholm tonight. Damn it, I've other things to do besides conveyor belt orders for you. And then I'm not allowed to get on with my work in peace and quiet but keep getting dragged to the telephone every other minute, so it's . . .'

'I'm sorry,' said Christer humbly. 'I really do apologize. But I really should like to know . . .'

'There's nothing much to tell,' snapped the doctor. 'The girl had a knife driven straight into her heart. It passed between the third and fourth rib on the left side without touching the lungs. The heart cavity was filled with blood and she died in a few minutes, probably about four o'clock in the morning. There was a brownish fluid in her stomach containing solid parts with signs of half-digested bread.'

'And what does that mean in ordinary language?'

'Coffee and buns,' replied the doctor laconically. 'Taken about two hours before death. Anything else?'

'Yes.'

'What?'

'You've looked at Norrgard, haven't you?'

'Only looked. I can't say anything until I've . . .'

'I know. I *know* you medical wallahs won't state hypotheses and theories. But surely you can, in the name of mercy, tell me if I'm an idiot not to close the case and persist in going on to find . . . a double-murderer.'

The other man was silent for so long that Christer was afraid he had gone away.

'All right,' he finally sighed. 'The man's got a mark round his neck which is typical of the usual kind on suicides who hang themselves, a mark that at the front runs horizontal but at the side of the neck runs obliquely towards the knot at the back of the neck. But . . . a careful examination shows signs of another mark, a more horizontal one, and lower down the neck. That . . . are you listening?'

'*Am* I listening!' said Christer, with emphasis.

124

'That mark is in my view more characteristic of *strangling* than hanging. A couple of other factors point in the same direction. With hanging there's squeezing not only of the veins of the neck but also of the arteries which take the blood to the brain. The face as a result is pale ... With strangling it is usually the veins which are squeezed, but the flow of blood to the arteries continues. Cause of death in this case is suffocation. The bleeding of the eyes and the blue colour or cyanosis of the face is nearly always present in this form of death. Do you see?'

'More than well,' said Christer grimly. 'So someone strangled him with a rope and then hung him up with the same rope from a tree. A clever and cold-blooded murder, which would have been perfect if you lot weren't even cleverer. But wouldn't it have taken considerable physical strength to strangle a man like that?'

'Not necessarily. Your unknown friend could have come up from behind and surprised him in his sleep, and once the noose was round his neck it wouldn't be easy to get free.'

'And when do you think it happened?'

'About two o'clock last night. But I must ...'

Christer put down the telephone receiver with a thoughtful expression on his face. He filled his pipe and leaned back to think. He knew that the solution was beginning to come within his reach. But there were still some things which needed weighing up and sorting ...

The quiet was shattered by the patter of high heels outside his door. Dina Richardson poked her brown head round the door and said cheerfully: 'Can I come in? I've come to make a confession.'

She was looking very pretty in a yellow dress and yellow shoes, and Christer's mood was distracted for a minute with pleasant thoughts on whether her brown legs were sunburnt or clad in nylons.

'A confession?' he said absently. 'That sounds interesting.'

She smiled at him.

'Yes,' she said. 'You see, I've not been completely ... er ... truthful to you, and I haven't liked that one little bit. I can

125

tell lies to the Inspector and if the worst comes to the worst to Leo Berggren, but not very successfully to you.'

Her soft voice was flattering, almost flirtatious. But Christer hardened himself.

'And why did you do so nevertheless?'

'Because I was so afraid of saying something which would put him in a fix.' She was twisting her handkerchief between her fingers. 'Yes, I know it was idiotic, but I really did think he had murdered Anneli. And whatever happened, I've still got a weak spot for him, and I thought I wouldn't make things any worse for him by gossiping about that I'd heard Anneli in his kitchen that night, the night she died. But now ... now everyone's saying that you've found the murderer and it was quite a different person, and so I thought ...'

'My dear Dina,' said Christer. 'What is all this about? Whose kitchen was Anneli in that night?'

'Len's, of course. And you must agree that it did look awfully suspicious the way he was so evasive and behaved so oddly and the suspicious things he gets up to at nights.'

She laughed lightly, amused at her own earlier anxieties.

'Last night, for instance, when he was pretending to be at home, sound asleep thanks to Doctor Severin's sleeping pills, what do you think he was up to then?'

And she added with a sniff of disapproval: 'Out in the car, that's what he was doing. Here in Skoga, too. Between one and two o'clock in the morning!'

Chapter Eleven

As Dina Richardson presumed that the culprit had been found and the case closed, she did not realize how dangerous to Len her testimony was. Neither did Christer enlighten her about the situation. He took the girl by her arm and piloted her more swiftly than in fact pleased her along the street and out to the tiny cottage in the summer colony area.

Len Larsson, armed with a garden hose and diverse cloths, was busy washing his blue Saab. He was highly indignant when he was asked to account for his night-time trip in the car.

'I most certainly wasn't out last night. I took those tablets at about half past eleven and—'

'Len, dear,' said Dina breathlessly. 'Don't lie to us any longer. They've found the man who killed Anneli, so you don't have to . . .'

He dropped the hose and stared almost wildly at them both.

'Have you gone completely mad or are you pulling my leg?'

'I swear it's true.' Dina turned excitedly to Christer. '*I* didn't take any sleeping tablets, and I was wide awake when I looked out through my balcony door and saw that car drive past. I was in fact rather mystified and curious, and then I lay and listened for it to come back. It returned about two hours later and perhaps I can be forgiven for speculating over the reasons for such an outing . . .'

'Stop a minute,' suggested Christer. 'Did you ever see who was driving?'

Dina looked surprised.

'N . . . no. I was upstairs and I only saw the roof and the back of the car. Do you mean. . . someone else might have . . .'

Len's sunburnt face was also sceptical and confused.

'But I locked the car, and I always keep the key in my trouser pocket.'

'And where do you keep your trousers?'

'In the cottage. On the chair there under the window.'

He stretched out his arm to demonstrate, but when it dawned on him how easy it was to reach almost anything in the microscopic room from the outside, he stopped and added uncertainly: 'The window was open of course. It has to be, or else one would suffocate from lack of air.'

'And you say you slept very heavily last night?'

'Yes, I was completely out. But to pinch the car key and go off with my car, that's really a bit much.'

Christer agreed wholeheartedly with him. It was a bold move but cleverly calculated if one wished to get up to the cottage and at the same time confuse any possible spectator. On the other hand it was the only possible story Len Larsson could tell, should he have risked remaining unseen during the trip and not been successful . . .

Christer Wick sat down in the long grass and nodded to the other two to follow his example. And there in the clover and the daisies and with Lake Skoga below him, he once again tried to extract the truth out of this singularly obstinate and recalcitrant witness.

'Why,' he asked, 'have you kept from us what happened here at your cottage on the night Anneli was murdered? No, don't give me that all over again. I can produce as evidence against your lies, several small important details; the lilies-of-the-valley by your wall, a hairpin on your kitchen floor, your coffee and your buns in Anneli's stomach, and in addition an observation by Dina . . .'

She lowered her shining brown head.

'Yes,' she mumbled. 'I'm sorry if it sounds as if I spend my nights spying on Len, but I suppose it's partly because he lives so near and partly because for a long time I've imagined that I'm in love with him.'

The young engineer flushed painfully, but Dina went on dryly: 'Don't worry, Len, I've come to the conclusion that it's a stage I've got over. In some way I think it's been a sort of Anneli-complex with me. She always was much prettier than me, and you had eyes only for her, and I just stood to one side and was envious and jealous. Then she got engaged to Kim and I hoped you'd forget her. I had a shock last Saturday

128

when I saw you were still mad about her and that in some peculiar way you were involved in her disappearance.'

She didn't look at either of them. Her fingers were pulling the petals from a daisy with nerve-racking deliberation.

'But then that evening, when you were drunk at the hotel, I was angry and at last felt free of you and indifferent to what you thought and what happened to you. To be really honest, I expect that had something to do with the fact that for the first time I felt attracted to another man.'

Christer watched with fascination as the white petals fell one by one into her yellow skirt.

He loves me . . . he loves me not . . .

'I couldn't sleep that night when I was alone. Someone was calling down by the lake and I thought perhaps you weren't feeling so good and needed help, so I decided to nip out and see. It was three o'clock and wonderful out – the sun out and the birds singing away at full blast. Well, I got here and then I heard you talking to someone in the kitchen. But the other voice, the one that replied – it was Anneli's! I went cold all over and I don't know whether I was more paralysed or angry or miserable. You two, who I thought were my best friends, up to something and leaving me out of it, cheating me . . .'

'For God's sake, stop.' Len beat the grass beside him with clenched fists. 'It was absolutely nothing like that at all. You make it sound like . . . like some kind of conspiracy.'

'What about,' said Christer gently, 'giving up all this secretiveness yourself and telling both Dina and me everything there is to tell about what happened during that busy day? That is, not little bits selected from what you were involved in, but *everything*?'

Len sighed.

'I've already told you practically everything. Everything except her visit to me that night. And I dared not say a thing about that because I was absolutely dead certain that you'd suspect me and arrest me for the murder.'

He turned accusingly towards Dina.

'Isn't that so? You'd discovered her at my place an hour before she was killed. And what happened? You were convinced I was the murderer. Didn't you rush straight here that

129

morning to try to warn me? "Be careful! They've found her now, not far away from here, so watch out." '

Dina said nothing at all and Len went on rather more calmly.

'I've been dragged into this mess by sheer chance all the time. It was pure chance that my car was parked in the street when Anneli rushed out into the rain. It was chance that I happened to be going up to the other side of the lake to fetch birch branches. And it was chance that I happened to wake up on Saturday night and went out on to the steps and saw Anneli. Though perhaps . . . perhaps there had been some noise which had woken me. I imagine she'd been talking to someone down by the shore. When I came tumbling out, thirsty and bad-tempered and my head aching like mad, she was standing over there on the big jetty, waving to someone out on the lake . . .'

'Matthew Norrgard,' said Christer quietly.

'That I don't know, for the sun was in my eyes and I couldn't see anything except a canoe. And anyhow I was much more interested in Anneli. I called out to her and she started and swung round and came up here.'

'What was the time then?'

'Practically three, I should say.'

'How did she look?'

'Well, she was wearing a nice white dress, but it was a bit crumpled. She had a few lilies-of-the-valley tucked in the belt – presumably those damned flowers she dropped here later on. No coat and no bag.'

'Her hair? Was it up or loose?'

'Up. She looked just as usual. Possibly a little more mature, a little older than usual in some way or other.'

'And what happened then?'

'Of course, I said at once, "Where the hell have you been and what do you mean by putting me in a fix like this?" But she just laughed and asked whether we couldn't go into the cottage—"if we're going to quarrel out here we'll almost certainly wake Mother up". Then she noticed that I had a whale of a hangover and she made some coffee while she got out of me what everyone had said when the wedding had been put off, and she smiled now and again, and now and again she said "poor Mother" or "poor Kim", and finally I lost patience with her and demanded some kind of explanation. But then she looked at me with those great big blue eyes of hers, which I never could resist, and said terribly slowly—'

He closed his own eyes and made an effort to remember her words and repeat them without embellishments.

' "Have you ever known a person betray you, Len? Not just anyone, but someone you're terribly fond of? Quite a lot of other things have happened too, but it was when I discovered this that everything broke. I'm terribly sorry that it has to be like this, but now that I can see the whole pattern, I can't do anything else." '

'Betray?' said Dina wonderingly. 'But who . . . ? Didn't she say . . . ?'

'Anneli never did say more than she wished to.' Len sounded suddenly tired and bitter. 'No. After that puzzling declaration she just smiled like the Mona Lisa, thanked me for the coffee and went on her way. And to be honest I was in such a state that I was quite glad to see her go. I saw that it would soon be four o'clock, cursed everything and everyone, flung myself down on my bed and went out like a light.'

'And when she left you, in which direction did she go?'

'She went along the path towards Lake House.' He rose abruptly and they could almost see the trembling of his nerves. 'All right, go on and say what you're thinking. After all, it's absolutely correct. *While I was sleeping off the booze, she was running straight into the arms of her murderer.*'

There was little they could say to this remorseful statement. And in as far as Len was to be relied on and could be written off as the murderer, it must have happened exactly in this way.

The question was, however, whether he really could be relied upon. Christer Wick spent the evening brooding over this and other problems. Helena Wick brewed jet-black coffee for him, functioned as telephone duty-officer, and otherwise left him in peace with his thoughts. Now and again she offered on request a psychological judgement.

'Yes, I realize that Len's many evasions and half-lies have

131

annoyed you. And it does undeniably look as if his tactics were to say as much as he was forced to say and to keep the rest to himself. But he's been put in a difficult position, what with his promise to Anneli and his loyalty towards her. Don't forget he was in love with the girl.'

'I'm not forgetting,' said her son. 'So much in love that he even might have found an outlet for his instinct to kill. He's abnormally violent, and I can well imagine him running amok when he saw that she — partly with his help — had sneaked off from her wedding with Joakim only to give herself to another man. Perhaps she told him, that night at the kitchen table, of her love for the wonderful Matthew. Perhaps they quarrelled and then he seized a kitchen knife which he had just used to cut the buns . . .'

'Christer, what a dreadful way of putting things.'

'Murder is dreadful, Mama dear. But I'd be glad to accept any other hypothesis . . . let's take it instead that his information is reliable and deserves attention. What one then has to face is first and foremost Anneli's own statement that she had been betrayed by someone of whom she was very fond. Betrayed in what way? And by whom? Now the person who betrayed her need not necessarily be her murderer, but in any case it's of vital importance to find out whom she meant.'

Helena Wick's dark eyes were unhappy.

'Anneli was a delightful girl,' she said hesitantly, 'but I would describe her as somewhat withdrawn and cool by nature. The people she allowed near her, of whom she was "very fond", can't have been very many. Gretel and Edward Strom . . . Joakim Cruse . . . And possibly Dina and myself.'

'From today on we must add to that list Matthew Norrgard's name. Though how a betrayal on his part could make her run away from her bridegroom seems incomprehensible . . .'

The longer Christer thought about it the more he was forced to admit that unfortunately there was a lot more than this that was incomprehensible . . . he had seldom had such an unnerving feeling of having all the available information at his disposal but being unable to piece them together.

132

The Tuesday went by without a glimmer of light showing in the darkness. He read reports, talked with Leo Berggren and fitted in a few new details into the confused picture.

A gang of youngsters, who had been waiting out on the lake for the sunrise on the Sunday night, read about what had happened up at the cottage and remembered that at about half past two they had seen a canoe with two people in it over by the north shore of the lake. It had been on its way towards the town. Scarcely an hour later the canoe had returned, this time with only one person in it.

And that meant that Anneli's activities were accounted for virtually up to the moment she had come face to face with her murderer. On the Friday afternoon she had disappeared from Len's car and made her way to Matthew Norrgard at the cottage in the forest. There she had stayed for the whole of the Saturday and not until the night after the wedding had she been taken back to Lake House by Norrgard. She had put her bag containing the freshly-picked lilies-of-the-valley down on the grass and waved goodbye from the jetty to the painter, who was then paddling away. This had happened at about three in the morning. At half past Sebastian came down to the lake after his amorous visit to Fanny Falkman. He saw a bag and a bunch of flowers but not the owner of the bag, who was at that moment drinking coffee in Len Larsson's kitchen. He also saw, however, a plastic headscarf and that proved that it had not been Norrgard who had deliberately taken it to hide it in the bushes up by the cottage. It had been put there later, by the guest who had also brought a piece of cut-off rope . . .

That this guest had made his way out to the cottage in a certain blue car was confirmed by a motor-cyclist who had passed the Saab just outside the town on his way home from a dance at one o'clock on Monday morning. A hurried investigation into the driving ability of those involved revealed that Fanny Falkman had never driven in her life and that Gretel Strom, although she had occasionally driven on Sundays, had not bothered to renew her licence. Dina often borrowed her parents' car, and Petren, Edward Strom and Joakim Cruse had their own cars. Joakim was considered to be a forceful

133

and highly skilled driver, who had competed in races occasionally and had even collected a few first prizes.

Reports also came in from the laboratories stating that there were no traces of blood on the knives or the clothes that had been sent to them. On the other hand the damp cloths from the wash-house showed signs of having been spotted with blood. They had been, however, too well rinsed to enable any analysis of the blood to be made.

The local police added yet another discovery. Inside the wash-house, which the murderer had evidently visited, there were several coils of thick clothes-line. But they had not been touched. The rope which had been put round Matthew Norrgard's neck had been stolen from outside Fanny Falkman's house.

'Yes, indeed,' said Fanny, when Christer went to see her in her shop. 'I had a very good clothes-line up in the garden. I'd done a huge wash the week before and then what with everything being upside down, I forgot to take it in. It was at least eight yards long and quite new, too. But people are quite unscrupulous nowadays. Sometimes it's as if they couldn't even *tell* the difference between what is mine and what is thine. Just imagine simply going into someone else's garden and carving a bit off a whole clothes-line just like that. Cheek I call it, and one might well ask . . .'

Christer nodded his agreement and then asked her sympathetically whether she had been exposed to any unpleasantness from the Misses Petren after the scene at the police station.

She snorted.

'What do I care about those two old hags. It's much worse for Sebastian. He's been having real old rows with them and that's not good for his blood pressure. He's worried about business matters too, so he's really had rather a lot on his plate all at once, poor thing.'

Christer suddenly realized that this red-cheeked florist now regarded him as a confidant, and he was not in the least embarrassed at making full use of this open-heartedness.

'Oh well, he needn't worry all that much about business, need he? Sebastian Petren is considered to be a wealthy man.'

134

Fanny shook her untidy head.

'Between you and me I think he's got mixed up in something rather involved. He's really down at the moment, and I should know better than most. And now some speculation or other he had on, which Edward Strom and that rich Mr Cruse were going to help him on to his feet with, has come to nothing, too, and he's ever so low about it. And you can imagine what a to-do there'd be in a town like this if one of the Petren family went bankrupt.'

'Has Edward Strom so much money,' asked Christer curiously, 'that he can help near-bankrupts back on to their feet? I've heard just the opposite said in the town . . .'

Well, Fanny Falkman did not really know anything about that, but Christer Wick was conscious of the fact that one of the more obscure points of this drama was connected with Petren's office and so he went straight to Edward and questioned him directly about it.

Edward scratched his greying head.

'Is friend Petren in difficulties?' he said in surprise. 'That's complete news to me. We do touch in some areas of business, but my business and income are pretty small fry compared with his. Gretel thinks I'm much too careful, but I prefer it that way, with a smaller and more secure living, to the ups and downs and roundabouts of high finance. I don't often do business with Petren, but in this particular case it was Joakim who brought up the suggestion that we should get together. I took it that Joakim, who has got a damned good head for business but hasn't any contacts in the timber trade, was willing to invest capital in exchange for my, and especially for Sebastian's, experience and our connections in the district. But nothing has been definitely decided on and now it seems as if Joakim feels inclined to back out of it. I regarded that as a natural result of his state of mind over Anneli's death, but if the same rumours have reached him that have reached you on Petren's financial position, then perhaps one should look there for the reason why he's backing out.'

'I realize that I'm being rather persistent,' said Christer, 'but I'd be grateful if you'd really search your memory over that conversation you had at Petren's office. What might you

135

have said that came as a surprise to Anneli and that upset her?'

'We . . . we talked about Joakim, of course, and amongst other things we mentioned our admiration for his business talents, but some doubts about his methods. I mentioned that it was said that he was as hard as flint and could make a dangerous enemy, but we weren't negative in any way, in fact on the contrary. Sebastian especially was delighted to be having him as a partner, and he joked about how useful it was of me to get hold of a millionaire as a son-in-law.'

Obviously no further progress could be made here. Joakim Cruse himself politely but definitely refused to discuss his finances with the police or give them any idea of the scope of his affairs. And Christer wondered, more and more irritated, whether he were not wasting his energies on inessentials, while the truth all the time lay hidden among the knowledge he already possessed.

Together with Leo Berggren he twisted and turned every single moment of the story, and they realized that after several days' work they were still not clear on the classic points of a murder case.

'Opportunity? Yes, they had all had an opportunity to murder Anneli except possibly Edward Strom, who slept with the easily-woken Gretel beside him. Weapon? Every one of them had had access to a strong kitchen knife, but why any-one of them should be running round the lakeside or in the wash-house with a carving knife in his hand is beyond my comprehension. And motive? If you can spot the murderer's motive then I'll give you fifty pounds of my next month's salary.'

Leo Berggren grunted.

'Well, two of them, the fiancé and the young admirer, had considerable cause for jealousy. The mother was angry and scandalized because of her daughter's behaviour. The friend was perhaps envious and jealous. The stepfather and her employer are more difficult—I can't think of anything special for them on the spur of the moment, unless Anneli had put her nose into something very questionable in the business line and they decided it would be safest to close both her nose

136

and her mouth. The florist I've long since given up. A woman who loves Sebastian Petren hasn't even the intelligence to commit two crimes.'

Berggren's calm and teasing voice rang in Christer's ears long after he had gone to bed, and all through a completely sleepless night he attempted to accept with the same equanimity as his colleague had, the fact that they were – anyway for the time being – completely stuck. But when this resignation did not manifest itself, he got up, lit his pipe and sat sunk in deep thought.

Gretel Strom had in her restlessness arranged Anneli's funeral for the Wednesday afternoon. The first half of the day dragged by. Everyone was uncomfortable and nervous. A violent change in the weather had brought with it rain and midsummer cold, which Christer found exactly in keeping with his mood.

The autopsy report did not succeed in cheering him up.

Apart from what he already knew, it appeared that Matthew Norrgard's body showed many signs that he had not died by hanging, but by strangling, signs such as the brain filled with blood, the bleeding in the membranes of the throat and lesser bleeding in the lung cavity and other internal organs.

Christer Wick's expression was grim as he changed into the formal clothes which had been intended for quite another purpose, and at his mother's side, he set off to the church. Despite the rain the streets were lined with people and there was a crush in the pews inside the church. But it was not simply an inquisitive congregation. The people of Skoga were both tactful and dignified, and their presence in such numbers at the funeral was a spontaneous and silent demonstration of compassion, a compassion which on this day without qualification or criticism, included both the stuck-up Gretel Strom and the outsider Joakim Cruse.

The candles flickered and the minister spoke warmly and simply of the two young people who had lost their lives in this tragedy, and as Christer looked at the white coffin with its lone bunch of lilies-of-the-valley on it, his resolution

137

hardened. The murderer of Anneli and Matthew could no longer go unpunished. Even if he were not certain, even if a great deal were still missing from the evidence he had arranged during the night, he must go into the attack and try to put out of action one of these black-clad mourners who at this very moment was simulating painful grief.

Or perhaps it was not a matter of simulation?

Dina's and Gretel's tears, Edward's and Len's obvious distress, Fanny's and Sebastian's emotion and Joakim's frightening pallor – perhaps they were all genuine?

Never before had a funeral seemed to him so long and so extended as this one. The ceremonies in the church, the car journey to the cemetery, the burial out there in the pouring cold rain, the melancholy meal afterwards in the banqueting-room of the hotel – it was all like a nightmare, which on his part was accentuated by the persistent torturing thought: Am I mistaken? Am I basing my case on too fragile evidence? Is it an innocent person I am watching and condemning?

And when the meal was at last over and Gretel suggested that the 'family mourners' should have their coffee at home at Lake House, he saw almost with fear that the circle, discounting his mother and himself, would consist exclusively of the people involved in the murder. After a broad hint on the desirability of Leo Berggren's presence, he manœuvred things so that he was also invited.

But the atmosphere in the green drawing-room at Lake House was extremely tense from the start. It was as if a gathering of black and white marionettes were making great efforts to swallow their coffee and speak a number of meaningless phrases. The rain beat against the window-panes and the electric light made them all look hollow-eyed and pale.

Not even Dina Richardson was at her best. She had cried too much and black did not suit her. Gretel's dress was all frills and pleats. Beside her the usually so vulgar and untidy Fanny Falkman looked refreshingly severe in her linen suit. The men were uncomfortable and unnatural in their formal clothes, Christer and Joakim alone wearing them with discreet elegance and naturalness.

Christer was too nervous to sit still. He placed his little gilt coffee cup on the marble shelf above the stove and thoughtfully studied the silent group of people in front of him. Tomorrow, he decided, when the worst of the funeral atmosphere had been dispersed, early tomorrow morning, he would visit one of the members of this company for a final questioning. He would give himself – and his opponent – half a day's respite. No more.

But suddenly the quiet was shattered as the nerves of one of those present finally broke. Her overstrained voice was the signal for Christer to intervene. Before either he or any of the others really realized what was happening, they found themselves in the middle of the final settlement . . . right in the actual unmasking ceremony. And when the starting gun had been fired everything came out with astonishing speed. To his own surprise Christer discovered that his brain was quite ready to reply to the desperate and hysterical question that was abruptly flung out into the room when Dina Richardson stood up and cried out: 'I can't stand it. Do you hear, I can't stand it. We all know it wasn't Matthew Norrgard who killed Anneli. The murderer is still alive! He's . . . he's in this room now. But who? For God's sake, Christer, tell us the truth . . . *Which of us is it you're after?*'

Chapter Twelve

THE impression of a marionette theatre became for several moments almost unbearably strong. The black figures stiffened on their sofas and drawing-room chairs, the coffee cups halted halfway to mouths and it was as if no arms could be raised, no tongues moved because someone had unexpectedly wrecked the ingenious mechanism.

Gretel Strom was the first to regain her ability to speak and move. Her soft doll-like face was confused, but she had grasped that one of her guests was behaving oddly and she was at once prepared to intervene within the limits of her capacity.

'Oh, Dina *dear*, you're shaking all over, and it's not really surprising when it was so freezing cold at the cemetery. And you're wearing much too thin shoes, too, just like all young people. But you shall have one of my crocheted shawls to put round you and then you'll feel better, won't you? Edward! Edward, dear, fetch one for me at the same time, will you? It really *is* a little cold in here.'

Dina sank trembling on to her chair and was wrapped in a bright red shawl, but her eyes did not leave the tall, pipe-smoking man over by the stove. Other eyes met his too – anxious, watchful, mistrustful.

'The girl is right, Christer,' said Helena Wick quietly. 'We'll all go mad soon if this weight isn't lifted from us.'

Christer's features were unfathomable.

'Have you thought that knowledge might be an even heavier burden?'

'I think,' said his mother, 'that the truth in a situation like this is always more bearable than the corroding unrest of not knowing, but thinking.'

'*The truth.*' Suddenly Christer sounded bitter. 'Yes, you're all expecting us to extract the truth from your incomplete stories and webs of lies. With the exception of yourself, Mama, who can hardly be said to be involved, there isn't *one*

140

of you who has been either reliable or honest throughout. Dina, for instance, was evasive and kept important facts secret to protect Len, Fanny Falkman to protect Sebastian Petren and her own private life, Len because he had made binding promises to Anneli, but also because he was obstinate and unco-operative and afraid of the police.'

Dina and Fanny flushed guiltily and Len Larsson looked as if he were finding his stiff collar too tight.

'And yet,' went on Christer, 'I have decided to believe just you three. In Len's case I have no choice. He is the one who gave the most interesting and enlightening information about Anneli's movements and her state of mind, and I must either presume that he imagined all this or I must accept his account. That I am inclined to do the latter is because, amongst other things, that in his account I think I have caught a glimpse of fragments of the pattern that Anneli had discovered, but which Len appears to be completely ignorant of.'

Christer had adopted his favourite attitude with his dark head thrown slightly back and his eyes fixed on the glittering chandelier in the ceiling, so he did not see how the young engineer brightened and at once returned slightly to his former candid and relatively uncomplicated self. On the other hand he was very aware that his audience had become extremely alert. Even Gretel in her baby-pink shawl was sitting absolutely still, and except for Christer's voice the only sound to be heard was the monotonous beating of the rain on the window-panes.

'The main point is and will remain, in my view, concentrated on the question: *Why did Anneli disappear?*

'Well, we know that on the Friday morning she received a message from Matthew Norrgard that he was expecting her up at the cottage where their short but obviously very intense love affair had taken place four summers ago. Personally, I imagine that Joakim's experiment with the bridal bouquet gave her a shock and forced her to search her feelings for the two men, so suddenly illuminated, and compare them with one another.

'But neither the letter nor the bouquet constitutes an

141

explanation for her behaviour. They were possibly the motive for going off in the car on the spur of the moment and then slipping off along the road to pay a last visit to the cottage. But not even her great passion for Matthew Norrgard could have kept Anneli up there for nearly two days and made her let down her parents, her fiancé and the whole of the town, all geared up to celebrate her wedding. Not if she was the kind of person you have all portrayed to me. Strong-willed, honourable, idealistic. A girl who was never precipitate, never went against the conventions, never was other than cool and balanced and controlled. What happened was that she suddenly behaved in a way which, according to your own unanimous statements, *was not at all like Anneli*. She herself seems to have been conscious of this. "I'm terribly sorry that it has to be like this," she said to Len, but she also said that she could not "do anything else". That does not sound like a defence of an unpremeditated and imperfectly-considered impulse.

'But what was it then which could explain how one lovely day in her twenty-fifth year she suddenly broke away from all her earlier standards of behaviour and shattered the whole of her existence?

'Well, according to the key handed to us by Len, something appalling had happened, something which caused everything to "break" for her and she discovered a pattern which drove her in panic into Matthew Norrgard's arms. "Have you ever known a person betray you?" were her very words. "Not just anyone, but someone you're terribly fond of?"'

Christer stopped to gather his thoughts, and the rasping of the match against the matchbox filled the room.

'Before I tackle the problem of what kind of betrayal and to whom she was referring, I should like to stop and consider a related problem. When and how had she discovered this treachery? It seems plausible that something happened during the course of the day. Despite the letter from Matthew she was obviously relatively happy and talkative during lunch. After that she was to try on her wedding dress and go to the hairdresser . . . What about it, Leo, have you contacted the dressmaker?'

'Yes,' said Berggren. 'She says that Anneli was there from twelve to twenty to one. She was friendly and pleasant and pleased with her dress and she asked whether Mrs Persson had been invited to the church.'

'The following fifteen minutes,' said Christer, somewhat emphatically, 'she almost certainly spent up at Petren's office. She was crying when she left there, and at the hairdresser's, where she arrived at one o'clock she was impolite and "quite absent-minded" . . . And now, gentlemen, I wish to know without any further procrastinations. *What was it she happened to overhear out there in the hall of that office?*'

Christer Wick's eyes were icy cold as they rested in turn on the three men.

Sebastian Petren.

Edward Strom.

Joakim Cruse.

His question had been swift and hard. Sebastian wriggled uncomfortably over on his green chair. Edward's forehead glistened with sweat. Only Joakim was sarcastic and unmoved.

'But my dear Chief Inspector! Hitherto I have had the greatest respect for your intelligence and judgement. But now you really have gone a little astray. I was most certainly not in my ex-fiancée's ex-office at the time you mention.'

'No,' said Christer dryly. 'But I have good reason to believe that you were present in spirit, if one can bring the concept of spirituality into anything as material as timber deals.'

Joakim shrugged his black-clad shoulders.

'I had promised my co-operation in a rather ambitious and not very well thought out transaction, and I withdrew in good time. What in the name of all timber merchants has that got to do with Anneli?'

'That is exactly what I want to find out. But I could hazard a guess. You are not a man to invest your money in uncertain enterprises. And the compensation this particular time was to be Anneli, wasn't it?'

Joakim's ears reddened slightly.

'You're insinuating something pretty horrible. So I was to

143

have attempted to buy my bride, was I? And Edward was to have sold her to repair his failing finances? Just like a bad nineteenth-century novelette.'

Sebastian Petren looked as if he were about to suffocate. But Edward managed a bleak smile.

'You credit me with far too much influence over Anneli. She was not one to allow herself to be sold.'

'Well,' admitted Christer, 'the expression is not mine, and it is unnecessarily crude. Let me put it so that I credit both you and Gretel with a great deal of influence over Anneli. She came to you to confess her wretched love affair; she almost certainly consulted you when another suitor appeared on the horizon, a suitor who was also a friend of the family. If I then presume that the suitor got you to put in a good word for him, that he with his fine instinct for business at once saw that Sebastian's and your finances were almost on the rocks, and waved before you the tempting prospects which eventual family ties might open, how would the picture look? I might add that he has said to me that he desired Anneli and was determined to "have her at any price", but that later he changed his mind and then hoped that she would accept him "with her eyes open and of her own free will". Out in the town, people are also sure that she did not love him but had been forced to become engaged to him by Gretel. I shan't say any more than that you may have been quite well-meaning in what you did and parents always consider that it's the best thing that could happen when their children marry money. But I imagine that the idealistic and romantic Anneli must have been deeply disturbed if she happened to have heard your own and Sebastian's cynical comments on the whole thing. You *have* got guilty consciences when it comes to that meeting in the office, and you've both been a little too eager to explain the episode of the keys and other details away. Now, tell me what you have to say for yourselves.'

And with unerring insight into which was the weakest link in the little chain, Christer pointed at the red-faced Sebastian Petren and said mercilessly: 'You can choose, Sebastian. Either you tell us all about it here and now, or we'll arrest you and make an official investigation into your affairs.'

144

Petren glanced unhappily at Edward Strom, but naturally chose to confess.

'Yes . . . ahem . . . well . . . you know what it's like when two men sit over a few drinks and don't know that there are any women about. One doesn't exactly watch one's words. And I'm hellish afraid I used that expression Joakim has just reacted against, when we were discussing how useful it would be to have a wealthy son-in-law. "You haven't gone and sold her to him, have you?" I said. And Edward grinned and said, "She has nothing to complain about. He's rich and pleasant and much sought after. Damn it, I only promised to help him get her as a bedmate, and I've done that." '

Gretel could no longer keep quiet.

'But Edward *dear*,' she exclaimed. 'You can't have been so *stupid* as to . . .'

'Don't interfere in this!'

It was the first time any of those present had ever heard Edward snap at his wife, and he at once added: 'I'm sorry, my dear. But this isn't the moment for digressions. We're all much too tense about what Christer is getting at.'

And turning to Christer, he exclaimed nervously: 'I repeat what Dina said just now. Which of us is it you are really after?'

So the question was put again, and Christer collected himself to give a definite answer to it. But he did not abandon the methodical thoroughness of his account.

'How much do we know now? We know that Anneli, on her visit to the office, had received a sudden and brutal insight into the scarcely idealistic world of men. She had heard that her stepfather had more or less acted as a procurer and that her fiancé had been prepared to buy her body for money. Both might well be interpreted as betrayal – anyhow from Anneli's rather more subtle point of view. And yet I don't think this is what she meant in her words to Len. Or shall I say, not only that.'

He at once began to talk more swiftly, as if he had now reached the central point and was conscious of the fact that the end was near.

'I want to tackle the problem from another angle, a less

145

psychological, more superficial and obvious angle. We have followed Anneli all through that day, from the florist's to the cottage, from the cottage back to the town on the Saturday night and on to Len's kitchen. There remains to follow her on the last stretch. When she left Len's cottage it was almost four o'clock. According to the autopsy report she must have died at about that time, in any case no later than five. Len saw her take the path which goes along the lakeside to Lake House, presumably at first to fetch her bag which she'd left down by the lake. *Where did she go then?*

'Did she meet someone down there or outside the wash-house? Naturally this is a possibility, but as the experts say she was killed with a strong knife of the carving-knife type, I should say this is not very likely. It is more likely that she met her killer indoors.

'Now there was one person with whom she was extremely eager to settle things at once. A person who had in his way treated her very badly, but who had been exposed to an even greater betrayal on her part. It is likely that she sought him out.'

Leo Berggren moved his chair so that he was sitting in the corner between the two doors of the drawing-room. Obliquely opposite him sat Joakim Cruse who, apparently undisturbed, was playing with his monocle. Without moving a muscle in his face, Christer studied the red head, the nervous, finely-cut features and the sensitive hands.

'Anneli's fingerprints and her hairpins were found all over your flat.'

Joakim smiled mockingly.

'Because of a certain Chief Inspector's arrival, the weekly cleaning of my flat took place on the Thursday instead of the Friday. On Thursday evening my fiancée had tea with me in my modest apartment and we tried out several different hair-styles to see which would be best for a bride.'

'Someone went through your door at about seven on Sunday morning. Where had you been?'

'Out for a walk.'

'And the black tie?'

'I never reply more than once to the same question.'

146

'Then neither will you wish to discuss king lily-of-the-valley?'

'As far as I'm concerned the subject is now closed. But I didn't know he'd appeared again, if that is what you mean. I only guessed. I had seen the lilies-of-the-valley in her hands.'

'Yes. And how did they get there?'

Another shrug. Leo Berggren wondered why Christer Wick did not lose his temper with this insufferable man. Instead he contented himself with smilingly achieving a perfect imitation of that superior and indifferent gesture.

'I can do as you have. I can guess. And basically it does not matter. What does matter is the fact that your flat is directly below my bedroom. And our nice old wooden house was not built so that one can undisturbed set about carving-knife dramas when there are people around. No, I'm quite prepared to write off the theory that it was to your lair that she turned her steps on that fateful night.

'But where did she go then?

'The answer to that question is as simple, as obvious and as natural as the answers to two other related questions.

'Why was the body lying just inside the grounds of Lake House?

'Why had the wash-house at Lake House been used to rinse out cloths and obliterate traces of blood?

'*Because the murder took place at Lake House*. Because Anneli, when she left Len's cottage, went straight back to her own home, presumably with the innocent intention of going to bed as soon as possible. And there in Lake House's well-equipped kitchen the murder weapon was only too easily within reach when she ran into the only person she might possibly quarrel with so violently that her hair came undone and her dress was torn. The person who betrayed her. The person whom she was so terribly fond of that for this reason alone she could neither understand nor forgive.'

Christer Wick did not give anyone in the drawing-room time to collect themselves after the blow. It was as if he wished to be rid of the operation as quickly as possible.

'I shall not torment you with too many details,' he said

147

almost coldly. 'Just tell me a few things. Did you clean the kitchen last Friday or last Saturday?'

Gretel's plump cheeks had turned the same colour as the shawl she was wearing. With her yellow curls and her china-blue eyes she looked like a miserable and wronged child. She nodded obediently as if with relief. This was something she could account for.

'Mrs Hansson scrubbed the kitchen floor last thing on Friday evening before she went. I was there keeping an eye on her, for she really *is* unusually careless and difficult.'

'But we found several of Anneli's hairpins on the linoleum. But you perhaps missed them when you . . .'

'Certainly not. Those hairpins must have got there after the floor had been done.'

'For God's sake, Gretel!' Edward Strom's voice was blurred and desperate. 'Christer, I forbid you to use her credulity in this way. She doesn't even understand what she is giving away.'

But Christer went on inexorably.

'And those kitchen knives, what about them? I thought you said you'd found them in the right place on the Sunday?'

'Well, of course, there was only the sharp new meat knife. I had washed it so carefully and put it *aside* on the cutting board on my table because I like to be a little *systematic* about the housework, but then when that policeman came and wanted to borrow it, it had been slung right at the back of the knife-drawer among all the other knives.'

'The policeman also asked you about some night clothes,' said Christer slowly. 'What clothes did you give them?'

'Well, it was my flowered one and a pair of Edward's blue-striped pyjamas. I always make several the same for both of us. One saves masses of material that way, and well, yes, there were my swansdown slippers and Edward's slippers, though he usually goes bare-footed, so they're . . .'

'And so you didn't have any dirty clothes in the house?'

'No, not last Sunday. I'd just got the laundry back and . . .'

'Are your other night clothes out in the linen cupboard?'

'Of course, it would have been much *nicer* if that constable had wanted to have them instead . . .'

'Thank you, we'd like to have a look at them, too, if you don't mind.'

Gretel Strom was quite cheerful at this stage, while Edward had become more and more grey in the face. She smiled in a friendly way at Christer and then asked: 'But what was it you said just then? About Anneli . . . and . . . and about Lake House. I didn't really hear properly and didn't really understand what it was all about.'

Edward's wide mouth twisted into a strange smile.

'No,' he said bitterly and yet gently, 'you don't understand anything you don't want to understand, and you don't listen. And so you're plunging us both into fearful misery.'

'But Edward,' said his wife in confusion, 'I simply don't understand you. I'm just being polite and considerate to Christer. You can't have any objections to that?'

'If he has,' said Christer caustically, 'then he can speak for himself. And first give a little lecture on sleep and sleeping tablets.'

Edward had straightened up his powerful figure and the two men's wills crossed and strained for the struggle to come.

'There's no point in your denying,' said Christer, 'that Anneli was killed here at Lake House. Too many witnesses have heard Gretel's admission about the hairpins and the freshly-scrubbed kitchen and about the meat-knife. It is also very easy to reconstruct the course of events. A quarrel, a stab with a knife in the girl's heart. Then panic. Where could one hide the body? In the lake, of course. And so the murderer carries her down to the lake. But either his strength fails him or it is the sunshine that frightens him. To row out and drop the body into the water would be much too risky. Perhaps Dina shuts her window at that moment and the murderer is terrified and flees. But the knife is part of the kitchen equipment. It will be recognized or missed and so it must be pulled out of the body and cleaned. The murderer himself has got blood on his hands and clothes and so he showers in the washhouse. His night clothes are a problem, but I imagine they are now in the linen cupboard among the clean clothes, while the police must be content with others which were worn after the murder.

'And now we come to the central factor in the whole of this mystery; the question of Gretel's sleep. It struck me from the very beginning as quite out of the question that Gretel, who slept so lightly, should not have been woken by what happened so close to her. Your bedroom faces the lake, *and even Dina heard Len call out to Anneli, although she lives so much farther away.* And although your kitchen is some way away from your bedroom and the house is solidly built, if one is sleepless and easily disturbed, then one is sleepless and easily disturbed.

'Why didn't Gretel wake up?

'Well, either *she did in fact wake up* when she heard voices outside the house, but for singularly serious reasons she wishes to hide the fact.

'Or *on that night as well she had been given sleeping tablets.*'

Edward smiled grimly.

'And in the first case Gretel could be the criminal, then? And in the second, I could?'

At last even Gretel seemed to grasp the horrible implications of this conversation.

'But Edward!' she cried. 'You can't let . . .'

'What happened, Gretel?' asked Christer. 'That evening after the cancelled wedding when you were tired and depressed . . . Did Edward give you anything to drink? Hot milk, perhaps, or . . .'

Gretel stared up at him with her eyes wide open.

'No, not at all. I only . . .'

'Be quiet, Gretel!'

Edward's furious exclamation cut off her words as effectively as if he had struck her.

'She won't say another word without a lawyer present.'

'That's not necessary either.' Christer's voice was lower and calmer, but it had a ring about it which made them all sit up. 'I know all that is necessary to know. I know which one of you two slept and which one was awake that night.

'The one who only pretended to take the sleeping tablets the next evening and so was awake that night, too, when Matthew Norrgard was murdered.

150

'The one who found the otherwise unknown cottage because he was the only person whom Anneli had told about Matthew and his romantic refuge. Perhaps he had been up there before out of sheer curiosity.

'The one who had the physical strength to overwhelm and strangle a grown man.

'The one who had the intelligence to plan and carry out an almost perfect crime; to hang a strangled man from a tree with the help of a rope which was not taken from the coils in the wash-house – a fact that might have pointed to Lake House – but which, as with the car, had been stolen from elsewhere.

'The one who after killing Anneli did not risk getting blood or other betraying marks on his slippers, because he was as usual bare-footed.'

Christer swiftly changed over to direct speech and continued implacably: 'Why did you say that the person who woke Gretel on the Sunday was Sebastian Petren "coming back from a fishing trip"? Our friend Sebastian here is not exactly the type to get up at the crack of dawn to get some exercise in the open air. No, but you had yourself been out and you'd seen him down by the lake at about half past three, and so it was the first name that came to your mind.'

Edward's powerful jaws clenched in defiance and desperation.

'All these are just loose assumptions and theories. Circumstantial evidence, not proof.'

'A sufficient number of them and sufficiently damaging evidence will do very well for getting a murderer a life-sentence in prison. And I have more. When Anneli heard Len describe the scandal in the town over the cancelled wedding, she said now and again, "poor Kim" and "poor Mother". Why not "poor Daddy"? She must have known that in such a situation it would be you and not Gretel who would bear the brunt of it all. And she was also, according to Gretel, more fond of you and confided more in you than in her. Why didn't she express any ordinary simple compassion for you, as well as for the other two? Well, I'll answer that question for you.

151

It was because *you had in a terrible way betrayed her confidence and at last she had realized it.*'

Edward's lips were so dry that he found it difficult to speak. But he was still not broken.

'And that "betrayal" was supposed to be that I had sold my stepdaughter's virginity for money, was it? Try convincing a modern court of the truth of that hypothesis.'

'Your more or less fishy money transactions are not the core of the problem, only a little part of it. "Now that I can see the whole pattern," said Anneli, "I can't do anything else." You had influenced her and persuaded her to accept Joakim's proposal, for her love for Matthew Norrgard was hopeless in any case. But you had done something much worse than that. To stop your plans for an advantageous marriage for her coming to nothing, *you hid or destroyed Norrgard's two previous letters to her.*'

Edward Strom's eyes began to flicker.

'That's . . . that's a damned lie.'

'You were nearly always the one who took in the post at Lake House. The first letter arrived in March, that is *before* Anneli had announced her engagement to Cruse. Matthew Norrgard wrote to say that his wife was dead and that at last he was free to approach her. Can you think of any possible reason why she should not have answered his letter? In one way or another, but anyhow answered it.

'Yes, Edward, there is one reason. Only one. *One cannot answer letters one has never received.*

'Why was she so terribly agitated when she received the letter from Norrgard last Friday? Because it was the first sign of life she had had from him since they had parted four years before. A month before she had denied to Dina that she corresponded with anyone in France.

'At the office she at last understood the connection, she saw "the whole pattern", and it is to her honour that she had the courage and initiative to revolt and break away out of it.

'When she returned home on the Saturday night, she found you awake. I presume you had given Gretel the tablets to get some peace and quiet to think about Anneli's disappearance and the consequences of it to your finances. You met out in the kitchen, and she faced you at once with your hypocrisy and treachery, and you quarrelled. You killed her—'

He was interrupted by Gretel. The pink shawl had slid off her shoulders and her blonde waves were disarranged. She turned towards Christer and her light tone contained a mixture of perplexity, fear and a kind of determination.

'I understand now. He got me to take two tablets because I'd cried so much I had a headache. But they weren't headache tablets but something which made me sleep while he sat up and drank whisky. Edward drinks much too much whisky, and he should stop doing it because it's bad for his liver. And then Anneli came home from that cottage up in the forest and Edward was jealous and drunk and mad and so he went for her.'

'Jealous?' said Christer in astonishment. He had considered many theories, but not that one.

Gretel nodded and it was impossible to decide whether her words stemmed from a surface thoughtlessness or from outrage of a deeply disappointed woman.

'He loved her. I knew all right, although he always thinks I never understand or notice anything.'

The silence was absolute.

His eyes rested steadily on the older man and he sensed that he was almost ready to give up. Leo Berggren passed a glass of water without saying anything. Edward drank it greedily and then mumbled hesitantly: 'I . . . I don't know. I find it difficult to see things clearly. It's true she attracted me with her youth and beauty and she wasn't of my flesh and blood, and I reacted to her presence much as other men. But I had no idea I was jealous until she appeared that night, blazing with her love. I was drunk and I was damned annoyed at what she'd done, and I called her a whore and hussy. And when she was ice-cold and superior and told me she had discussed me with her lover and he had advised her to tell Gretel and Joakim everything and eventually the police, too, I went mad and hit her. Then I tried to kiss her and she grabbed a knife from the table and was going to defend herself with it. We struggled . . .

153

And then . . . well, then everything was all over in a few minutes.

'I took her down to the lake but was frightened by some noise at Richardson's and so I left her there. I pulled out the knife and so that I shouldn't get any more blood on me, I wrapped it up in the bit of plastic she had in her bag. I rinsed the plastic later but I was afraid that fingerprints would still show on it, so I didn't dare throw it away. I took it with me when I went up to the cottage the next night and put it there to mislead someone.

'I knocked on the door of the cottage and when the painter came out, sleepy and confused, I threw the rope round his neck and pulled. It . . . it was almost horribly easy.'

'But why?' began Christer.

And Edward mumbled indistinctly: 'I *had* to. You see, I had never even thought of killing Anneli. It was the whisky and our quarrel and the struggle, and then the knife which I twisted out of her hand, which made it all come to a head. But before she died she had revealed that both she and this Matthew Norrgard knew too much about me and my activities to be really pleasant. And I realized on Sunday that as soon as you got hold of him, then his testimony would be enough for you to solve the problem of who it was who had a reason for murdering Anneli.'

He had been sitting with his grey head bent, but now he raised his eyes with an enormous effort and looked at Sebastian Petren, who looked away at once, and at Joakim Cruse, who met his eyes with sympathy and compassion.

'As I'm trying to be honest and make things clear, I'd like to add one thing. It wasn't just that Anneli had seen through my shabbiness and betrayal of her. During her unfortunate visit to the office she had heard much too much about my doubtful and shall we call them sanguine affairs. She herself used a more discriminating expression. I must relieve Sebastian of all responsibility. His affairs are fairly involved, but he is not dishonest. It was I who tempted him into deeper and murkier waters. One *can*, if one is very smart, buy bad forest land and sell it as good land. One can, in fact, in special cases, even sell timber which doesn't exist. Sebastian was uneasy

154

and muttered during our conversation about enticing Joakim into something dubious. And I said cynically that people like Joakim could stand most things, and we must take this chance to salvage our finances and escape bankruptcy and police enquiries. It was in connection with this that I happened to mention that Joakim wouldn't make a fuss whatever happened, as he was willing to pay a high price to go to bed with Anneli. And Christer is perfectly right when he says she was deeply hurt and upset over my betrayal and my amoral callousness. She threw it all in my face, point by point: how I'd accepted her confidence over Matthew and yet kept back his letters, how I had consciously tried to marry her off so that I should benefit, how I kept up a façade of financial honesty and respectability while I was planning crooked deals and downright illegalities, and finally how I had shown up my true nature when I had even made physical approaches to her. She did not want to understand or even forgive me. If I hadn't stopped her by force, she would have rushed straight into the bedroom to tell Gretel . . .'

Edward Strom fell silent for a long time. So long that Christer wondered whether he were not going to continue. Then he turned to his wife.

'But I did not want that,' he said simply. 'She could threaten me with Joakim and the police; I could perhaps stand that, but neither she nor her damned snooping lover under any circumstances was going to worry you with my approaching bankruptcy or bother you with my drunken attempt to kiss her. For even if there is something in that I was much taken with her, you are profoundly wrong in one important respect. It's you I love.'

Dina was sobbing quietly. Leo Berggren, who had long been dreading the moment when he would have to arrest a good friend and fellow chess-player, glanced uncomfortably at Christer.

Edward Strom suddenly broke. His hands shook so that he could hardly fill the glass with water, the sweat poured down his white collar and the pained furrows in his broad face deepened in an almost uncanny manner.

But Gretel Strom showed both her limitations and her

strength in this difficult situation. She did not weep, she did not have a nervous collapse, she simply rose from her place and took her husband by the arm.

'I suppose,' she said gently, 'they have to take you with them. But you can't go in those clothes. I'm sure they're terribly uncomfortable and impractical. Come, and I'll help you pack . . .'

An hour or so later, when Edward Strom and Leo Berggren had already left, Helena Wick looked into the drawing-room and told her son that she was going to stay at Lake House with Gretel.

'But,' she added, 'she'll get over it. And she hasn't a word of blame for the man who killed her only child. She's asking now how often one can visit and send parcels to the prison. She's a remarkable woman.'

'Yes,' said Christer repentantly, 'I'll have to take back what I said about no one telling the truth. Gretel Strom is truly an exception. I simply don't believe she's capable of inventing a lie. Goodnight, Mama, I hope you both sleep well . . .'

Fanny Falkman and Sebastian Petren left, too, a plump elderly couple, at present somewhat subdued and crushed. Christer remained standing in the green room and watched them leave.

The tragedy is over, he thought, and the actors are leaving the stage.

He himself felt intolerably weary.

But when Dina put a last question, he collected himself to reply to it.

'Tell me, that bunch of flowers which Anneli took with her down from the cottage and which she had in her hands when she was dead . . .'

'Yes?'

'Was it really Edward who took them out of her bag and put them there? Somehow . . . it . . . doesn't seem like him.'

Christer caught Joakim's eye.

'No,' he drawled. 'I'm pretty certain it wasn't Edward. The flowers were, just as the bouquet on the coffin was, an apology

156

and a romantic gesture. A courtly acceptance of the "dream of the lilies-of-the-valley".'

Dina smiled in some consternation. But Len thumped her impatiently on the back.

'Come on. It'll be nice to get some fresh air after all that.'

Joakim held the door open politely for her.

'I thought perhaps,' he said, 'that I could come for a drink at your parentless maidenly castle. That combination seems to be much more tempting just now than fresh air . . .'

Dina hesitated for a second. She was standing between the two men, the one fair and untidy and rather childish, the other slim and monocled and mocking. Her scarlet shawl flared against the black background. She was very pretty.

Christer Wick knocked his pipe out slowly against the stove. Of the feelings which filled him, fatigue was undoubtedly the least disturbing . . .

They walked side by side along the street in the pouring rain.

And the small, silent and omniscient town observed them watchfully.

Another sensation to add to the previous one?

She had a hundred wrinkles on her nose when she laughed.